While You Were Gone

Kate Moretti

While You Were Gone
Copyright © 2014 by Kate Moretti. All rights reserved.
First Print Edition: July 2015

ISBN-13: 978-1-940215-52-5
ISBN-10: 1940215528

Red Adept Publishing, LLC
104 Bugenfield Court
Garner, NC 27529
http://RedAdeptPublishing.com/

Cover and Formatting: Streetlight Graphics

For Lily and Abby, chase a passion.
Anything you want. It's important.

DEAR READER

While You Were Gone is a stand-alone novella based on the novel *Thought I Knew You.* It is, simply put, another side to the story. It's not the same story, but if you read this novella, you will know the end of *Thought I Knew You.* You'll know what happened to Greg (I think that's okay, but you should know this going in).

When I published *Thought I Knew You,* I expected a certain level of conflict over Greg, Claire Barnes's husband. Some readers told me they didn't know why Claire would ever keep him in her life (in any regard). This didn't make sense to me. *But Greg is not a bad person*, I said. *He did a bad thing.* To me, these are obviously divergent character traits. *But he's a good father, sometimes a good husband,* I'd insist. It wasn't always good enough.

No story is one sided. No person is all good or all bad. Those split-second decisions, driven by loss, insecurity, grief, or anger, these are the decisions that interest me: the ones that don't live in the black and white. The mistakes. The human-ness.

While You Were Gone is my attempt to make Greg and Karen human. Lovable, even. Despite their mistakes.

Thanks for reading.

Kate
July 02, 2015

CHAPTER 1

NO ONE LIKES THE CALL that comes in the middle of the night, the one that jolts you from the deepest sleep and sets your heart racing. If you're getting that call, someone is either in jail or in the hospital. Maybe someone you vaguely remember loving has been kicked out of Tig's bar. Again. Their keys have been taken away, and they are sitting on the front stoop, under a drooping awning and a blinking Miller Lite sign, with a fat lower lip caused by either fist or fall. And if you're me, that someone is your mother, which is ridiculous and embarrassing. Then again, Paula's never been one for subtlety.

I don't want to go. I've gone the last three times, and it's Pete's turn. I listen to some idiotic Nickelback ring-back tone, as though my brother isn't thirty years old with a wife and three kids under five and is instead a sullen high school sophomore with pocked cheeks and an addiction to angsty pop music. Maybe I'm a tiny bit bitter to be the one getting this call. Why doesn't Tig ever call Pete? Oh right, because he never answers.

His voicemail clicks on, and I leave a hasty message. "Hi. Needed you. Paula is at the bar again. Thought maybe you could go this time? I have an early-morning violin audition. Hello? No. Got it. Typical." I slam the phone on the nightstand and shove my feet into brown moccasins that Paula got me for Christmas last year—maybe two years ago. Last year, Paula bought us scotch.

I throw on a sweatshirt and snatch my keys off the hook. I consider bringing her here, letting Paula sleep it off on the couch. I picture the condition of Paula's house: frozen pizza boxes and empty liquor bottles balancing on top of the garbage bin. Last time I was there, I pointed out a collection of mouse droppings in the pantry, and she waved me away with an irritated sigh. I'd bet money they're still there.

Cold air whips around my face and my neck. It smells like bonfires and marshmallows, the way November air should. Clean and fresh. I climb into my faded blue Toyota and turn the key. The engine brays and gasps, and for a moment, I think I'm going to have to call Pete back or maybe even the police. Eventually, it turns over with a grumble that shakes the whole car.

I cut a U-turn right and check the clock: 3:15 a.m. I know that whatever time I pull into that dusty parking lot spotted with gleaming Harleys, there will be a fight. The bars close at four, and even a moment before is too soon. I'm mostly past the point of humiliation, but every once in a while, it sneaks up on me, and my stomach coils while I think, *this is my mother. This is not the way this should be going down.*

I expect her to be sitting on the front stoop, but she's not. The parking lot is surprisingly empty, and the music from inside isn't the typical country twang but an electric rock, loud and garbled, sung live with shitty equipment.

Paula sits hunched over a tumbler of something clear, smoking a cigarette in the far corner of the bar. She's talking to the guy next to her, who looks my way when I walk in. She glances up, sees me, and rolls her eyes. She shouts across the bar at Tig.

"You know, Tig, one of these days, I'm gonna stop coming here. Every time I let a little loose, you up and call my babysitter." Her voice is rough cut, and she coughs. I stop two feet from her and give her time to get herself up. She looks me up and down, a small sideways smirk on her face. "You mad, baby girl?"

"Well, it's three a.m. I have a nine o'clock audition tomorrow. I've been... happier."

She stands up slowly, trying not to stumble, with slow, deliberate, underwater movements. She actually looks good, my mother—tall and skinny like me, and her highlighted dark bob angled against her face is slick and trendy. She doesn't look like a woman falling apart. She's aged well. We could almost pass for sisters, a fact that delights her to an embarrassing degree. She brings it up to strangers,

3

to people at the movies behind the popcorn counter. *Some people think we look like sisters. I'm her mother, you know. Crazy, right?*

She picks her way to me. It's only a few steps, but she stumbles, her right ankle turning. Instinctively, I stick my arm out to catch her. She's as light as a child. She leans against me, sneezes, and I realize her cough wasn't nicotine fueled.

"God, Paula. Are you still sick? Have you been to the doctor?" I'd talked to her last week, and she'd coughed a blue streak into my ear. I'd asked her to see someone, but she brushed me away, *too busy.* Doing what? I can't even fathom it.

She giggles and taps her finger to the bridge of my nose. "Look at you. It's like you're my mama, not the other way around." She perks up and holds her index finger an inch from my face. Her eyes go bright, and she wriggles away from me. "I'll be right back."

I watch her sashay across the room, her narrow hips swinging, and I follow her, a dutiful puppy. She leans in to a tall, good-looking man closer to my age than hers, planting a wet, lingering kiss near his ear. "You come back again, soon, okay?"

He laughs and hugs her back. I look over at Tig, who is drying a glass behind the counter, and he shakes his head at me. Humiliation hits, which, in turn, sparks a surge of anger. My mother coils herself around this cute stud of a man, who either doesn't realize that she's closer to sixty than forty or doesn't care. I march up and grab her elbow, hard. Her face whips around to mine, her eyes narrow, and her mouth bunches like I'm a kid playing under a clothes rack while she's trying to shop. *How dare I?*

"We're leaving," I announce, and I see Tig out of the corner of my eye, paused in his toweling and watching us carefully. My mother can be explosive, all sticky-sweet pecan pie, with that sugary, almost Carolina accent one minute. Then boom. Her anger knows no limits. I remember the long fingernail scratches weeping fat drops of blood down my father's arm. He wrapped a towel around his arm and cursed at her, *Goddammit, Paula.* She ran around, clucking and preening, administering antibacterial cream and bandaging—apologetic to the point of being almost gleeful. No one but me was surprised when he left.

I yank her arm harder. "Now." She follows me out, waggling a finger wave to the remaining patrons.

I jerk open the passenger-side door and push her in.

"Ouch, Karen. That seems unnecessary." She pouts, dramatically rubbing the spot above her elbow.

I climb in the driver's side without a word, and she pokes one manicured finger into my bicep. "You know, you didn't have to come. Tig overreacts. That's all."

"But you can't drive, and God knows Pete won't pick up, so it's me."

"Well," she says reasonably, but it comes out like

Welllll. "Pete has a family." An accusation. I am less because I do not.

At her house, I pull up in the driveway. The garage door is caving in, the soffit sinking, rendering it useless. It's been a few months since I've been back. I guide her inside and direct her upstairs, where she strips out of her clothes, leaving them tossed around the floor like a drunk college kid. I follow behind her and gather them up, smoky jeans and a white billowing, gauzy shirt. I roll it all up in a ball and shove it in her nearly empty hamper. All around the bathroom and bedroom, clothes are piled in bunches. There must be three loads of laundry alone on the floor. I gather it all together and push the mountain in front of the hamper.

Paula crawls into the creaking old bed and lies flat on her back, immediately closing her eyes. She pulls the covers up to her chin and keeps perfectly still, pretending to be asleep out of spite. She looks dead with her sickly pallor and whitish-blue rings around her eyes.

I kiss her forehead. Her lipstick feathers in all directions, caked in the lines around her mouth. She smiles, placated, and pats my hand.

"You might make a good mother one day, Kay-kay," she whispers.

I flick off the light and leave the room, slipping the door shut behind me. Downstairs, I survey the kitchen. In the sink teeters a tower of plates and mugs that are surely days old, crusted and yellow.

The countertop is dull with the residue of unknown substances, dotted with brown coffee rings. The lid to the trashcan lies on the floor next to the garbage, and a cinched bag sits on top of it. Next to the sink, a half-eaten apple is clouded with fruit flies. I pitch it in the trash, tie up the whole mess, and dump it out back.

I text a message to Scott: *Call me when you wake up. I'm at my mother's. Story later.*

I roll up my sleeves and let the hot water run over my hands until they scald. Using the abrasive back of a sponge, I scour the countertop, working in small circles until the sweat drips down the back of my neck, and I hear Paula's whisper in my ear.

"You might make a good wife someday, too."

I am twenty minutes late the next morning, and the empty chair to my right mocks me for the whole four-hour rehearsal. Amy Sung, third-chair violinist and the closest thing I currently have to a best friend, avoids me. She rosins her bow in a meticulous rhythm at breaks and speaks in hushed tones to Nikolai, the conductor. I try to catch her eye, but her gaze slides one way, then the other, off to the side, or unfocused against the far wall. I feel it. She'll compete. She's auditioning, too. I am the natural choice: I have the years of experience. Although I'm young, I have the technical expertise.

I'm already assistant concertmistress. But nothing is guaranteed. My stomach pits.

The Toronto Symphony Orchestra has low turnover. It's the full stop at the end of a long, winding career filled with teaching positions and lesser orchestras. There's nowhere else to go. Except first chair. Concertmistress. In my six-year term, I've seen that first chair empty one time, for four days. Until Lesley Maxx.

Lesley played in the TSO for fifteen years, and her retirement was expected—celebrated, even. Most professional musicians retire long before sixty, but Lesley stayed sharp and quick with the bow. Her eyesight and ear never wavered. When I asked her why she was leaving, she patted my shoulder. "Always leave when you're ahead. The alternative is pity."

I attended the banquet. As the assistant concertmistress, I gave a speech, appropriately teary, for the woman who had become my mentor. I cried when we hugged. She tucked a lock of hair behind my ear, kissed my cheek, and whispered, "It's all done. You're a shoo-in." I assume she spoke to Nikolai. She spent the banquet night guiding me through the crowd. "Have you met Karen? She'll be my replacement." And those within earshot laughed good-naturedly. She was serious, though they didn't know that. They thought she was being tongue in cheek, tossing it out of the side of her mouth like a vaudeville joke. Sure, I'd have to audition, but what Lesley said went. The queen speaketh. The minions obey.

Even Nikolai kowtowed to Lesley, who had twenty years' experience on the next senior member of the TSO. She had demands, and he'd grudgingly scramble to meet them with ineffectual mumblings. She might have been a diva, but she drew a crowd. If Lesley said I was her replacement, I was. Easy peasy.

"Am I good enough?" I'd questioned only once, and she'd rapped the top of the music stand with her heavily ringed hand and brayed, a snort of rough air from the back of her throat.

"You're better than you think, and that's your biggest problem."

In music—like most things, but somehow, I thought, especially music—a lack of confidence could kill you. It renders your notes weak, your timing off as you second-guess yourself, kills your passion. Anxiety was a known exterminator of all things passionate.

My confidence with the bow, even after almost twenty years of training, was a subject of discussion. Nikolai, Lesley, Amy, everyone has opinions, things I should or shouldn't do. Have faith in myself. Play for a recording. Audition for a solo. I have a tendency to end weakly, the sound lilting and dipping to its final conclusion. I'm easily thrown by an imperceptible squeak, a periodic eighth beat, a too-late entrance. I routinely have trouble recovering.

"A concertmistress must, above all, lead," Lesley

admonished me time and time again. My neck and ears burned.

I am chased by one sinking, sickening thought: *I'm not good enough, and I have no idea why.*

I fumble through rehearsal, nerves skittering across my knuckles at the pending audition. My end notes are weak, sputtering, and insecure. My hand moves woodenly, not fluid, and I shake my wrist out between pieces. My eyes burn, thick and sandpapery behind the lids.

"Are you okay?" Amy taps my shoulder. Those are the first words she's spoken all rehearsal.

"I'm fine. I had to go get my mom at Tig's." I press the pads of my thumb and forefinger into my eye sockets, and the pressure, for a moment, serves as a relief valve.

"Again? You just got her, what? Two weeks ago?" She forgets to be weird, or whatever game she was playing before, I suppose the one where she doesn't tell me she's going to audition against me in an hour.

"Three. Yes. No one calls Pete. He has a family. He doesn't answer. I *do* answer. Ergo, Tig calls me. Every time." I take a long drink of water, and Amy leans her violin against her shoulder and gives me an awkward one-armed hug.

"I'm sorry, Kar. Can I do anything?" She pauses then picks at her thumbnail.

"Are you going to audition for concertmistress?" Being tired sometimes makes me reckless, or at least less able to tolerate someone else's bullshit.

She levels her gaze. "I am. It's fair."

I consider this. She's right. Yet I clutch the edge of my chair until my knuckles turn white. I want to throw the bow. First, I want to snap it over my knee, and then I want to throw it, all wildly pinwheeling across the stage, held together by the hair alone. I want to see everyone gape and duck and whisper. I want to, for once, lose my shit. I want to be the one with problems, the one no one can rely on.

Instead I smile at her. I tell the truth, even as it hurts. "Sure. That seems fair."

I have Lesley. Amy is older than me by five years, but she has less orchestra experience than I do. Besides, I'm a shoo-in, so says everyone.

In front of my stand, I feel the string of tension pulled tight across my shoulder blades. Every movement is forced and unnatural. I can't help thinking it's because I'm so damn tired. The back of my throat itches, and I fumble through the last movement. The piece I'm so familiar with, Bach's *Partita No. 2 in D Minor,* seems foreign to me. The easy, light dips and valleys and skips feel heavy and drawn out. The melancholy lilt bends dense and slightly flat, even to my own ears. I overcorrect and cut a few notes short. Nikolai arches his eyebrows and sets his lips in a straight line.

"Passion is a thing you chase, by chance or choice," Nikolai says, his tongue curving around the Ss in his vague, expansive accent. "Passion isn't a solid thing you can hold or tame or put in your purse and take to dinner, stroke it like a rabbit's foot or a feather dream catcher. You can have it and lose it in the same piece, the same moment. It can seep away from you as quickly as water down a drain once you pull the plug."

As my bow arches and stretches across that final note, a three-count D, I can tell I've chased it. I'm breathless from trying to catch it. Damascus nods once, a curt businesslike acknowledgement. An A for effort. Lesley hovers in the back of the auditorium and gives me an encouraging smile. The doors open, and a threesome clatters in, all whispers and giggles: the Sung family. Amy rushes to the back of the auditorium, just as Nikolai clears his throat and calls back, "Closed-door audition, please."

Amy ushers them back out the door. I picture her mother, a short blunt cut, sleek against her chin, and her father, slight, with intelligent eyes and her sister, just fifteen and wanting her big sister's life— her mother's and father's pride.

I swallow the caustic bitterness that has lodged itself in my throat. My mother, once that stage mom, reamed out a conductor for a youth orchestra for cutting me when I was ten. He'd laughed at her, and she'd brought her boot heel down, hard, on the toe of his dress shoe. I search my memory for his criticism. I was too stiff, he said. Too practiced.

I almost laugh at the memory. To be followed by the same critique your entire career is an accomplishment. I clasp the violin case shut and hover backstage. Lesley has disappeared, not wanting to be seen blatantly playing favorites at the audition, I surmise. There are two other violinists to hear. I could stay. I contemplate it as I move toward the back of the auditorium in the dark. In the lobby, I can hear the Sungs giggling. I could go say hi, exchange pleasantries, ask Mr. Sung how the veterinarian business is. I think of my mother, her one leg hanging off the bed, fully dressed but asleep, the run in her pantyhose ending in a gaping hole around her big toe, the wet air puffing from her mouth stinking like gin.

Amy chooses my other standard audition piece, another one of Bach's *Partitia,* in E major. It's light, quick, and her bow flies over the strings. Agile. Adept. The first five minutes is a show of skill until the notes deepen and slow to an emotional lilt. She hovers at each note a fraction of a beat longer than she should. It's a risk, playing off the sheet like that, almost as if she's trying to highlight my tendency to be technically on point. I exit the side door into the frigid March afternoon air. I don't need to stay.

The wind slaps at my cheeks as I walk the full two miles home. The violin case strapped to my back bangs as I walk, puffing air out through my cheeks. My lips burn from being chapped. I pass Faraday's Pub, and from inside, someone shouts a garbled word, and the sound of a crowd's laughter floats out the front door. I consider going in, marching up to the bar, lining up a few shots. Being that person. Just for a moment, handle it the way Paula would.

My mood is black, the kind of hopelessness that makes you kick stones and mutter under your breath. I pull my phone out of my pocket and call Scott, but it goes to voicemail. I fumble with my cell, trying to shove it in my pocket.

I turn the corner onto my street and fly straight into someone, a man holding a folder of paperwork, reading as he walked and clearly also not watching where he was going. The papers go flying, scattering like leaves in the wind, and I'm at once apologetic. I grab as many as I can. We both kneel on the ground.

I hand him everything I could gather. "I'm sorry. I wasn't watching. I've had a stupid, terrible day. I was lost in my own head." I watch a few of the white sheets skip and flit down the street. I contemplate chasing them, but frankly, he wasn't really paying attention, either. If he wants them, he can chase them.

"It's fine. I don't really need it anyway." He stands up, straightening what he's been able to salvage in the folder, and gives me a sideways smile. The sun glints off his glasses, giving him a penny-eyed look. He rubs his chin. "I've been meaning to go paperless…" His voice trails off, waiting, I suppose for some laugh, a girlish giggle.

"Sorry again." My phone vibrates in my pocket, and I wave as I walk away, fumbling to answer before anyone hangs up.

"Wait!" he calls after me. "I'm looking for a place. Do you know where, uh, Faraday's is?"

"It's right on this street. About two blocks down. You can't miss it. Sounds like there's a real party in there." I motion quickly, hot to get to my phone.

"Thanks." He hesitates then waves good-bye.

I fish my phone out of my jacket, and the screen shows one missed call: Scott. I return his call and get no answer. I grunt in frustration. It's been less than a minute. Where did he go?

I let myself into my dark apartment and rest the violin on the chair. Without turning the lights on, I pull a fleece blanket to my chin and curl into the corner of the couch. It is five o'clock on a Thursday night, and I have nowhere to go. There is no one I want to see, except for my somewhat-absentee boyfriend, who makes only half-hearted attempts to see me as of late. I call him one more time, just to make sure, but the phone rings twice and goes to voicemail, as if he rejected the call.

I should call my mother. I ought to wait for Nikolai. I could call Amy.

I do none of these things. Instead, I sleep.

CHAPTER 2

I NCESSANT BUZZING PULLS ME FROM the deepest reaches of sleep. I don't recognize it as my doorbell until I'm up, foggily pushing my hair off my face, where it has stuck in dried wetness on my cheek. My left foot radiates a dead buzz, having been tucked under me while I slept. I check my phone. It is nearly midnight.

I creep up to the door and peek through the peephole. Scott. He hits the buzzer again and runs a hand through his black hair. I yank the door open.

"Where have you been?" I ask, my mouth still sour and stuck.

He gives me a weak smile. "Hey, babe. I tried to call you."

I look at my phone and see four missed calls. "I must have passed out. I had to go get Mom from Tig's last night. I was up all night." I turn and make my way back to the couch, pulling the blanket closer around my shoulders. I flick on the table lamp, and the room instantly illuminates in a soft, cozy glow. Scott sits on the cushion next to me, but he doesn't relax, lean against me, fight for his section of the blanket. Instead, he perches like a waiting bird.

Scott and I met at a jazz concert in Woodbine Park more than four years ago. We had both dragged reluctant dates: his, a girlfriend, a fledgling relationship, precariously resting on mutual attraction and a shared like of caramel mocha cappuccino. Mine, a first date, a bored jock. A mistake. At the refreshments tent, we'd each ordered a complicated drink, his for his girlfriend, mine for me, and sat waiting off to the side, making small talk about the bands, our favorite jazz musicians. He'd seemed utterly shocked I knew anything at all, and I had teased him, *Why? Because I'm so young?* As though I didn't have every Coltrane CD or couldn't debate stylistic differences between Dizzy Gillespie and Fats Navarro. I left him, my drink in hand, his jaw hanging open. Later, he spotted me in line at the Port-a-potty and asked me for my number in what he later proclaimed as, "the creepiest thing I've ever done." He couldn't leave me there, he said, rotting and unappreciated by some rugby player who thought that jazz was the instrumental top-forty Muzak played at Chinese restaurants. I gave it to him, of course, in a rush, both of us red-cheeked and flushed from the furtiveness of the whole thing.

At first, our dates were thrilling, a rushed talkfest comparing jazz styles. New Orleans versus Kansas City. Big Band versus Blues. Avant-garde versus soul. Scott was in a jazz band, and I went to see him play, all glassy eyed and ruby love. Later, backstage,

I jumped him, his sax still around his neck, the horn digging painfully under my armpit.

Somewhere along the way, we stalled. No, that's not right. We petered to a slow hum, meandering here and there but without an engine. I liked jazz, loved it even. Scott lived and breathed it. He even taught it, a high school music teacher and head of the Jazz Club. His enthusiasm for classical music was less. In the beginning, he'd gone to my concerts out of support. He said he didn't understand how I could deal with so much structure. *Didn't I have passion?*

I lean against him, forcing the fix. I'm not willing to let him go. We're dying, but I'm willing to give CPR one last time. His hair is dark, almost black, and his mouth full and sensual. I once asked him what the girls down at the high school thought of him. I could see them, falling all over themselves for one last rag on that sax, those big gorgeous hands working that brass. He'd rolled his eyes and elbowed me off him. He probably loved every minute of it.

He kisses the top of my head, and I pull his face against mine. I think of my mom then Nikolai, his mouth in that firm, straight line, telling me what I already knew, and I wrap my legs around Scott.

"I've had a shitty day. I'm glad you're here." I nuzzle into his neck, and he smells clean, like soap and aftershave. "First I had to get Mom. Then I cleaned her apartment because honestly, it looked like a disgusting mess. She's getting worse. Next, I blew my audition." I work my fingers up into his shirt, moving against the warm fuzz of his belly. His hand claps over mine, and he pulls it from underneath the fabric.

"Kar, I need to talk to you."

"Is this about last week?" I sit back against the back of the couch, folding my arms across my chest. We were over it, weren't we? It was a stupid fight. Everyone has those.

I'd pushed things, as I usually do. We'd been together for four years. We should be thinking about the next steps, at least moving in together. I think I said it in Paula's voice. Later, I wondered if I was so desperate to please a woman who would never quite be pleased with me that I'd managed to shove that responsibility onto the shoulders of my boyfriend.

"Do you really want to live together?" he'd asked. "Why?"

"It's the next step. Are we going anywhere?" I was a sitcom cliché. Worse, a soap opera one.

"I like our life. We work. We have crazy schedules. I do the jazz club on some evenings. I like how we're together when we choose to be, not because we have to be." He faltered. "Is it the money?" I had thrown my coffee mug at the wall behind his head.

Now, he moves his hand across his chin, the stubble making scratching noises against his palm. "No, it's not *exactly* about last week. But it made me think, that's all. Are we going forward here?" His dark, brown eyes are bloodshot and red rimmed, and I see with sudden clarity all the signs I've missed.

I've been so royally stupid. Him showing up here at midnight wasn't because he desperately needed to be with me or was worried about me. It isn't even a booty call. This is a break-up conversation. My arms goose bump. I shift to the right, putting some distance between us.

"Are you speaking hypothetically?" I won't make this easy for him. I'll make him say it outright.

He sighs. "No, Karen. I'm not. Do you think we're going anywhere?"

"Did you hear me earlier when I said I've had a truly terrible day?" I don't want a pity relationship, but later, when he feels guilty, I'd love it if he remembered this.

"I did." He eyes me in his peripheral vision. "I just feel… compelled."

"Compelled."

"I can't sleep, lately. I feel like we're doing this thing to each other where we're only… surviving."

"What are you getting at, Scott?" I know what he's saying, but I need him to actually *say it*. He's a big fan of beating around the bush. In fact, his first *I love you* had a twenty-five-minute preamble.

"We should be more to each other by now. We should be engaged or married, or hell, at least passionately resisting those things for the sake of bucking convention."

Passion. That effing word again. "We aren't? You seemed to passionately resist moving forward last week."

"No. I said I liked our arrangement, and

you agreed. We just agree on everything. It's maddening, really."

Even now, his voice is even, and I feel only a minor tug of *something somewhere*. Mostly, I am pissed because this is how my day is going to end: with us agreeing to break up, the way some couples agree to share a chicken parmigiana at a family-style restaurant. He's right. We don't fight. Aside from that one fight last week, our most heated arguments have been about jazz.

"So you're saying that because we agree too much, we should obviously break up." I curse myself for giving him the out. I said the words "break up" before he did, thus filling in any blank for myself. He never had to say, "I'm breaking up with you."

For a moment, I want to be that girl, the one who screams and cries and begs to be friends, thinking instead that I can change him, turn him from friend back to boyfriend. I want this to be hard for him to walk away from, these four years, a waste of my prime marriage years, as Paula would say. I am not that girl, although I am the girl who will throw a thing or two, should I get really angry. The problem is, this whole *break up*, which he still hasn't confirmed, doesn't make me really angry. I guess in that way, I concede his point.

I study his face: the soft hollow under his cheekbone but above his jawbone, a pillowy, concave spot I've kissed countless times. His too-large ears and the way they redden at the tops for hours after he's been in the cold. His permanently swollen saxophone lips, smooth and ridge-less from years of vibrating against a reed. The mole that hides under his sometimes too-long sideburns. His dark eyes. His long, girlish eyelashes.

I prod my emotions—looking for sadness, grief—but come up empty. I think of how I'll never feel those lips, those large hands, again. How the last time we made love was actually the last time, and had I known that, I might have paid attention instead of composing a grocery list in my head.

I take his hand, pull it against my stomach, and he tilts his head. He leans forward and kisses me, long and slow. I wait for the thump of my heart, the racing that maybe used to happen, but who knows when it stopped. I wait for the breathlessness. I wrap my ankle around his ankle, more out of curiosity. Will he take one for the road? I wonder then, almost irreverently, if I should, knowing it might now be a while? Could I keep him if I tried? I almost laugh into his mouth.

He pulls away, gently, with a smile. "This is the right thing, Karen. You know that." He says it with such conviction—more than I've ever heard from him really—that something inside me clicks.

"There's someone else." It's a wild guess, but as soon as I say it, I know I'm right.

"No." He's quick to reply, which confirms it. Scott is never quick with anything.

"Yes. There is. Who?" I'm again driven by

curiosity, not hurt, which should be the biggest red flag, but I don't take the time to consider it. "Who is she?" I press, inching closer to him. I touch his arm.

"Karen. Don't." He shifts away from me, his jaw set.

"Scott. You owe me this at least. Tell me. Who?"

"Just. No one." He stands. I jump up and position myself in front of him, studying his face.

"Rosalita. What is her last name? Juarez? The art teacher. Spanish girl. Small waist, curved into wide, round hips. High heels. Young." I'm almost teasing now. "You like them young." I am six years younger than Scott.

He looks decidedly uncomfortable, and I know I've hit the mark. I've been to enough retirement dinners and school functions to know most of the teachers. I'd caught him and Rosa chatting a little too closely more than once. When I interrupted at the buffet table, they'd jumped apart like I'd thrown a dead mouse between them.

"What does she have that I don't? That we don't?"

He rakes his hand through his hair and pulls it straight up. "Karen. Stop." His voice is rough, but I can't stop.

"I feel compelled," I say snottily. "Tell me, and this whole conversation is over."

"She gets me, okay?" He throws his hands up in the air, a rare loss of control.

"She gets you," I repeat dumbly. "I thought I got you. Jazz, Coltrane versus Davis. I get you, Scott."

"That's not all of who I am. Jazz doesn't define me. I'm more than that."

"You're a deep well." Meanness is my go-to. He shakes his head at me like I've disappointed him somehow. He steps forward into my space and hugs me. It's so unexpected that I feel my eyes well up. I don't want to cry for him, especially not in front of him. We stand there, in the middle of my dimly lit living room, for what feels like forever. I wonder if they're a thing, he and Rosa. If they've done this, gently swaying to some inner music. Scott always has inner music, a deep, soulful bass line in his head, waiting for the right notes, the right be-bop or scat. What I've been missing, Scott has always had in spades. *Passion.* I wonder if Rosa has that, if she's a hot-burning stereotypical Latina with her art and her easels and her paints and her cleavage, while I was black-and-white measures and rests and decrescendos. Waifish blonde.

Scott thumbs my chin. He kisses my cheek. I walk him to the door. We say good-bye. It's all very anticlimactic.

He's gone.

I should sleep restlessly, tossing and turning, the sheets tangled up in my feet. But I don't. I sleep the sleep of the dead and wake up late yet again. My back is stiff from lying in the same position all night.

I race to rehearsal and fall into my chair at five

of nine, which is technically on time, although it's later than everyone else. Susan Post leans over to Amy and whispers, "Congratulations," and I notice the cardboard box of roses next to her chair with a large, enthusiastic card: *We're so proud of you!*

Before I can assimilate all this, Nikolai leans over me, sucking his teeth and rocking back on his heels. "Karen, my office?" My eyes dart from the clock back to his lined face, and he shakes his head. "No matter. We'll start late. This is important."

Nikolai's office is lined with bookshelves, and his desk is large, ornate mahogany. I've been in here a few times, and I've always felt squeezed, as if the walls are a vise. It's small, cramped, and filled with odd sculptures, statues, talismans.

"Karen. You left. And you were late this morning." His voice is soft and filled with reproach. "Not the behavior of a leader."

I chew on the inside of my cheek. He's stating a fact. I say nothing but sit up straight and pick a small fuzz off my skirt.

"Why? Were you afraid? Angry?"

"Yes." I blurt. My plan was to stay silent, say nothing, nod gracefully. But he hits a nerve. I am afraid. I am angry. I am all of the above. "Amy got it, then?" I have the presence of mind to clarify before I rant and rave.

"Yes." He leans back in his chair, studies me, like this is some kind of trap or a test that I'm destined to fail. He reaches up on his shelf and pulls down a white, single-tusked marble elephant statue, mounted on a gleaming black platform. He holds it out across the desk as though it's a piece of paper, and when I take it, one-handed, I almost drop the whole thing, it's so heavy.

"What is this?" I narrow my eyes. Nikolai is famous for his glib, Delphic comments, given at any moment, especially during rehearsal and auditions. A citizen of the world, he likes to call himself, born and raised cross-continental, his accent a mishmash of Russian and something vaguely Middle Eastern. He quotes Buddha and the *Tao Te Ching* with equal regularity but is also likely to season liberally with verses from the Quran and the Bible.

"A white elephant is a well-known symbol of Buddhist strength. I have my own version. The one-tusked. Strength in the presence of adversity. Eh?" His face cracks in an almost-smile at his cleverness. I palm the heavy thing and stare at it. Its marble eyes gleam at me, almost mocking. After my past two nights, I'm not in the mood for enigma. I think of how Scott would love Nikolai, had they ever met. There is likely a reason we broke up.

"Okay." I gently place the elephant on my lap and wait.

"You are a tough cookie, Karen." He says this like *tooof coooookie. "*You have been through a lot, no?"

I shrug, because *a lot* is relative. Compared to whom?

He raps his desk with his knuckles and continues

without waiting for my reply. "Ah, well. What do you say to that, right? Okay. Here's the thing. You have technique. You are respected by the group. But something in you… You are not ready to lead. You are too young."

"That is bull," I interject and palm my eyes. "You are the one who said that age is just a number."

"I'm not talking about your age. You are too unsettled right now. You read music. You play music. You don't feel music."

"I'm the best violinist in Toronto. Or all of Ontario. Maybe even Canada."

"I'm sure. Technically, I'm sure." He nods, bows his mouth down, and scratches his cheek.

"Then what? Nothing about this makes sense to me."

"That's your problem, Miss Caughee. You think the world makes sense. You don't see any beauty when it doesn't."

"You have no idea what I see," I say quietly. I gently place the sculpture on his desk, on top of a manila folder with my name on it, and I leave him there, stroking his chin with his sad, strange little smile. I head to rehearsal.

Because I'm a professional, I head directly to Amy's chair and tap her on the right shoulder. She turns and cocks her head, questioning.

"Congratulations. I'm happy for you, but I need a few days. Okay?"

She nods and gives me a twist of her mouth, almost a smile. "I'm sorry I hurt you, Kar. Really."

"Are you sorry you auditioned?" The question slips out before I have time to think about it.

She hesitates and studies her violin in her lap. When she looks up, she squares her jaw and takes a deep breath. "No."

I call Pete and almost fall over when he picks up. I'm stomping my way home from rehearsal, skipping the cracks in the sidewalk like a kid. Nikolai's voice fights for space in my head over Mom's, over Lesley's, over Scott's. *You are too unsettled. You might make a good mother one day. Are we going anywhere? A concertmistress must, above all, lead.* My stomach feels empty, scooped out, but my heart stutter-skips in my chest, an irregular, angry rhythm knocking against my ribcage like a kid kicking a pebble.

"Is it Mom?" Pete replies when I ask him to meet me for dinner.

I push aside a trace of annoyance. "No. It's me. Is that so impossible to everyone?"

"That you'd need me? Um, maybe?" His voice edges up but breaks when he laughs. "Sure, I'll meet you for dinner. Lemme run it by Mindy. I'll call you if anything changes."

Mindy. I picture her face twisted in annoyance as she balances two kids, one on each hip, and a third tugging at her pant leg. Her perfectly lined lips, her tightly pulled hair, nary a wisp out of place. Even her yoga pants are clean. She's a "together" mom, which is why it sometimes makes it so hard for everyone to believe I am barely a "together" person. I wait for the cancellation phone call, but it never comes.

At five-thirty, I push open the door to Faraday's, and the smell of wet wood and cologne slaps my nostrils. Faraday's is largely a businessman's bar, but I like it for the Reubens. Pete is fifteen minutes late, which lets me take the edge off with a quick martini. A group at the end of the bar is watching soccer and laughing, ties undone, unbuttoned at the neck, jackets draped in a pile across the back of a chair. They all seem to know one another with a familiarity that comes with working together for years, and they elbow and mock each other like brothers. I have no idea what that kind of friendship feels like, and the realization sits in my gut, doing a dangerous little tango with the liquor.

"Hey now, Shortcake." Pete slides into the booth across from me and gives me a grin. The childhood nickname feels good. I've missed my brother. "What's the matter?"

"Nothing. I can't just want to see you?" I pull a Sweet 'N Low pack from the cut-glass holder and flip it around my fingers.

"You can, but you never have. So I thought this was about Mom?" He pushes his glasses up on his nose. My big brother, almost five years older than me, looks all of about twelve years old. He has sunny blue eyes, sandy hair, freckles across his nose, and a dimpled smile. Mindy generally leads the pack, Coach diaper bag in tow, and Pete trails behind like one of the kids. I've rarely seen them apart.

"Sort of. She was bad the other night. Her apartment... we have to talk. What do you want to do? Have you seen it?"

He shakes his head. "I know I need to go over there. She said the dead bolt needs to be replaced, but I thought maybe she lost the key again."

"I can't be the only one doing this, Pete."

"I know. But I have the kids. I work. I don't know when I'm supposed to be Mom's keeper too." He tugs on his ear and looks around for the waitress. It should feel more wrong to talk about Mom's alcoholism while sipping on my third martini.

"I don't know, Pete. But it can't be all me. She hasn't done laundry in weeks. Her pantry is empty except for tuna fish, and I swear she doesn't take the trash out. There're mouse droppings."

He sighs. "Yeah, that's bad. I get it, Kar. I do. I just... there's only twenty-four hours in a day. Mindy is going nuts with the kids by the time I get home, and the twins just started ballet. Apparently, they're virtuosos. Is that the right word?" He digs around in his pocket for his wallet, flips it open, beams a smile at me. "Look." Two chubby four-year-old ballerinas stand in second position, side by side. Identical blond pigtails. Serious blue eyes gaze into the camera. They look like Pete, minus all the pink. I push the wallet out of the way.

"Yeah, they're cute. I agree." I throw back the rest of my drink as Pete rolls his eyes. "I need to come over and visit my nieces. But we really need to figure this out, okay?"

"The blind leading the blind," he mutters. The waitress appears, and we order drinks, Pete a beer, me another martini, and sandwiches. She brings back the drinks, sets Pete's pint in front of him, and he checks his watch when he thinks I'm not looking.

He takes a long swig of his beer. "Here's an idea. I usually get off early on Mondays. Why don't I go to Mom's and fix her dead bolt. I'll look around the house and get back to you. Then we'll plan some kind of intervention, okay?"

"This Monday." I twirl the olived toothpick around my glass.

He tips his head and gulps his drink. His phone buzzes, he reads it, frowns, and taps a quick reply. Then he looks back at me blankly. "What?"

"This Monday. You'll go this Monday?"

"Yes. This Monday. I'll call, and we'll talk, okay?" He stands up. "I'll get mine to go. We have a plan. Mindy just texted. One of the twins spiked a fever."

"Wait, Pete. I…" I look around helplessly. "I've had a shitty day. Can't you stay?"

"The kids are sick, Karen. I'm sorry, I would. But…" He gives me a half smile. "You'll see one day. I don't have time to think about my shitty days

31

anymore. They're all just... days." He tosses a twenty down on the table and gives me a perfunctory kiss on the cheek. "I'll call you Monday, okay?"

He pushes out the front door through a thick, gray-suited or khaki-clad crowd. I survey the bar: two groups of men on either side and a lone bartender drying glasses with a dishtowel. I migrate to the center of the bar and offer a weak smile to the bartender, who nods back.

"Another?"

"One more, then I'm out. Going home." I suck on the olive, tangy and sweet, and absently watch the television.

"Going home? You're the only one in here worth talking to." A guy hovers to my left, the kind of guy that romance novels would call dangerously good looking. Dark hair, dark eyes, chiseled jaw, black jacket. I side-eye him and try not to smirk. Truthfully, he smells like pine and something wonderful, and I half want to fall for it all. Faraday's is where a local girl can go to get hit on, picked up, and anything else her little lonely heart desires. I flash on the image of a guy, this guy, in my bed, between my legs, kissing my neck. Where Scott used to be. I inch closer.

"That guy who left you here is a jerk." He leans in, and his face is inches from my face. All our little face electrons jump around, making sparks.

"You're right. He is a jerk," I agree. The leather from his jacket brushes against my hand. My fingers tap against my elbow. I give him my best "rescue me" face, batted eyelashes and pouty lip. I think about how much fun this can be, this little stupid game, and how I forgot about that. With Scott around, I haven't really played it in a while. My mood fizzles out like flat pop. I straighten up, lean back, and give Leather Jacket a smirk. "He's also my brother."

"Well, brothers can be jerks, too." He shrugs, his smile edging up higher on one side. "I have a sister. I bet I'm a jerk sometimes."

"I don't doubt it. Listen, I'm not really the best company. This was fun, meeting you, if that's what you call this. I don't know your name but—"

He extends his hand. "Mike Potter."

I take it reluctantly. "Nice to meet you, Mike, but I think I'm about to leave."

"Really? So soon?" He stands up, his back against the bar. "Listen, I'm going to run to the little boys' room. I'll get you one more drink, and when I come back, we can start over. Just talk." He holds up his hands. "No come-ons, I swear."

"That is actually a come-on. Just so you know."

He motions for the bartender to get me one more drink—which is one more than I promised myself I wanted ten minutes ago—and trots off in the direction of the bathroom. Who the hell says "little boys' room"? A free drink is a free drink. Oh, my God, I'm my mother.

"Pay no attention to Mikey. This is what he does. He's a 'God's gift' kind of guy." The guy is leaning against the bar, sorting peanuts into small piles. "I mean, to be honest, it generally works for him. I guess I don't know if it'll work this time or not, but he's rarely brushed off."

"I wasn't brushing him off. I've just had the world's shittiest day. Normally, I'd play along."

"Okay, you go first. 'Cause I think I can beat you." He's cute. Average. Glasses and a nice smile. Smart eyes, where you can tell he's watching the world behind those glasses, even though they look like—

"Hey, I know you." I almost say *penny eyes* but stop myself. He's the guy I ran into in the street, knocked his files over.

"Yeah, I know. You ran into me the other day." He ducks his head, a small smile playing on his lips before he redirects his attention to the hockey game.

"I'd call it a mutual... crash. But, yeah." I stab the olive at the bottom of my glass and bite it. "So tell me your day. I bet I win."

"This is like the worst happy-hour conversation I've ever had." He leans back, and his full smile is nice. Wide and friendly. "Okay, so the other day, when I packed, I did a terrible job, which is crazy because I travel constantly. I should be good at this. But I forgot"—he ticks it off on his fingers—"my toothbrush, my razor, extra boxers, and my lucky tie. Also, I forgot my notebook, which I carry everywhere, that had all my flight info in it. So, fine, I use the kiosk and my phone like everyone else. But I can't tell you—I was thrown. Then I get stuck on the plane next to a guy coming from backpacking

Eastern Europe who spends the whole two hours detailing how toxic our lifestyle is, particularly deodorant and toothpaste. Then I get here, and I'm told I need to teach all new material, only later to discover it's all executives. So I'm studying the class content after Day One, only to come around the corner and be railroaded by a woman who is clearly not paying attention, and half the class information, including the roster, goes flying off, halfway across Toronto. So today, I have to teach this class, no roster, no notes."

I'm laughing. I can't help it. "Wait, so those papers were all you had? It's 2011. You must have it electronically."

"No, no, no, Greg here is old school." Mike is back, his hand clamped on Greg's shoulder. "He does everything on paper like it's 1985. Even his khakis have pleats."

"I think I can beat this. I really do." I clear my throat. "I had to pick my mother up from a bar, drunk at three a.m. I auditioned for concertmistress of the TSO and didn't get it, against my best friend, who did. Now we're not really on speaking terms, which may or may not be my fault. My boyfriend surprised me at midnight just to break up with me, and my brother has pretty much left my mom for me to handle because he has a 'life of his own.'" I use air quotes with my fingers. "My career is shitty. I'm not sure I'm a good violinist anymore. My relationship is over, and I'm just truly lukewarm about the whole thing. And my mother acts like she's in college, even going so far as to pick up guys my age. Mike, are you paying attention? Do you like cougars?"

"Who doesn't?" He tosses the remark over his shoulder as a big play on the TV above our heads sets the crowd roaring.

"Mike is an equal-opportunity offender."

"Offender!" Mike protests, turning his attention back to me. "Were you offended?"

I shake my head. "No, I'm just... tired. Ready for bed." The line of bar taps swims in my vision. *And drunk.* The TV pulls Mike's attention again, leaving Greg and me to sit in silence.

"You know," Greg starts and pauses. "My mother was an alcoholic. She died years ago, and she had other problems. Mental health mostly, a touch of schizophrenia. But she always had a bottle of vodka open and going. Mixed with anything, really. OJ, AJ, Coke. I didn't realize it until I was older, but she was."

He goes back to sorting his peanuts, and I can't figure out his system from where I'm sitting. I don't know how to respond to his admission. Should we trade alcoholic mother stories now?

He talks before I can. "I'm sorry. I don't know why I told you that. In fact, I don't think I've ever said that out loud to anyone, ever. But, there you go. The truth comes out in weird ways."

"No, I'm glad you told me." I touch his arm, and he stares at my hand. I pull it away. "I'm sorry.

I'm sorry about your day, and your papers and… your mom."

"Well, I think you win, anyway." He rubs his hand back and forth across his chin. "Your day was pretty awful."

"Do you ever…" I feel the words slosh around in my mouth, my head. "Do you ever want to be someone else?"

He stares at me for so long that I wonder if I've said them out loud. It's possible I just thought about saying it. I stand up, the din of the bar gaining volume, and I can't hear myself. I like the happy-hour crowd. I'm not up for the nighttime and the men like Mikey with their pick-up lines and wedding-ring tan lines.

Finally, Greg speaks. "Only every day."

"Maybe not someone else." I'm swaying now, my purse over my shoulder. My tongue feels thick and heavy. "But someone who actually is first-chair violinist. With the perfect boyfriend. And a circle of friends. A brother who cares. A mother who… is a mother. I don't want to be someone else. I want…"

"To be the very best version of you," he finishes softly. His eyes meet mine, warm and brown, and his mouth curves up, his nose wrinkling slightly at the bridge. "Yeah, I get it."

"How do you be that best version of yourself? That's exactly it. Those are the perfect words." My voice is louder than I want it to be. I inch closer to him until we are a mere foot apart. I smell his spicy hotel-soap smell, and our breath mixes in the air between us.

"I don't know how. I just try, every day." He stares at me intently. "All we can do is try. We can't control anyone else. For instance, wayward running girls who don't look where they're going."

"It's just the perfect thing to say," I repeat and feel stupid. The alcohol is fighting its way back up my esophagus, and I don't want to vomit on his shoes. I stare into his face, his perfectly *nice face*, with his penny eyes, little white glints of light off the glass. I imagine carefully removing his glasses so that I can see his real eyes, velvety brown. I imagine my hands on either side of his face. His mouth on my mouth. "I should go."

I sway into him, and he grips my elbow. "Let me walk you out. Are you okay?"

"I'm destined to be Paula." Drinking brings out the melodramatic side of me. "Yeah, I'm fine."

"May I walk you home?"

I shake my head. It's only half a mile, but I don't want to walk it. I'm tired, and I'm afraid if I walk it, I'll spend the entire time crying because I can't get it together. I don't know why I feel like crying. I was fine fifteen minutes ago. I pull my cell phone out of my purse and speed dial the cab company. They give me a ten-minute wait time, and I hang up.

"It was nice meeting you, Greg." I offer him a watery smile.

"It was nice meeting you... but you never told me your name."

"Karen. Karen Caughee."

He takes my hand. His palms are hot. "Are you sure you're okay?"

I nod. "I'm fine. Sometimes it all catches up with you, and then you drink. Then you cry. I guess maybe that's a girl thing."

"I think there are guys who drink and cry." He smiles, takes my arm, and leads me outside. The air slaps my face, and the wind bites at my cheeks, my chin. We wait for the cab.

"My mother wasn't always an alcoholic." I kick my toe into the soft gravel at the edge of the sidewalk. "My father left, maybe ten years ago. Sick of her craziness. She was always up and down, but it was after that when she started drinking." I babble, not knowing if I'm defending my mother or complaining about her. "But he was no angel. He was a drunk, too. I'm doomed."

Greg reaches out, touches my shoulder. We stand like that, a foot of distance between us, his hand on my back, resting warm and comforting between my shoulder blades. Without thinking, I lean up on my toes and press my lips to his. It feels the way I thought it would, warm and soft, like chocolate chip cookies straight from the oven, like fires and thick blankets on a rainy day. His mouth moves a little under mine, unsure and hesitant. My fingers curl around the fabric of his jacket and pull him tighter.

The cab pulls up. Greg leans back and gives me a confused look, clouded eyes and knitted brows. I climb into the back seat. He leans down to the open window.

"Be careful, okay?"

I nod, and the cab pulls away. I watch him on the sidewalk and wonder if I should have given him my number or asked him for his. I know that I've never really met someone who I thought could maybe, possibly see me, right down to my soul, as though I wore it like a patch on my shirt, a blinking shiny thing: *this is me, all that I am*—which is such a stupid way to think. I met a man for forty minutes in a bar and had one very nice, close conversation with him. Shared one drunken kiss that I can still feel, twitching all between my thighs and curling my toes. Somehow, that conversation has wormed its way into my body and squeezed around my heart. I wonder if it's possible for a person to fundamentally change who you are, even if you only knew them for less than an hour. Because as ridiculous as it sounds, his words rattle around in my brain. *The very best version of you.*

We're stopped at a light. The light flicks green, and we pull into the intersection. Greg stands on the sidewalk, his hand raised in a half wave. I'm still watching him watch me when I hear it. The squeal, a scream. I turn my head just in time to see headlights, glaring and white in the window, closer than they should be, and coming toward me very fast. A sickening, horrible, loud crunch. When I look up, the sidewalk is sideways, and Greg is running, his mouth open. He's yelling, his hand waving in the air. My ears flood with fluid, but I can't hear anything. I feel drunk and tired and wonder why the car isn't moving. There's more screaming.

Everything goes black.

CHAPTER 3

"**H**ELLOOO! YOU'RE AWAKE!"

I struggle to sit up, pushed back by a tangle of tubes and a thick, cottony fog. "Was I not awake?" I try to ask, but my tongue gets caught up, tangled in the words and too fat for my mouth.

"Oh, you have some bruising, but you'll live, I swear it. You've been sleeping for a while."

She smells like peaches, a tacky, cloying Yankee Candle smell, and her acrylic nails clack together as she untangles the wires. My eyes follow the plastic lines right into my arms—well, one arm. The other is wrapped and suspended in a sling that hangs from the ceiling. My eyes trace the outline of my body under the hospital sheet and land on my leg, balancing much in the way my arm is. I'm in traction. I remember the cab, the screeching, the screaming. The man running. I realize it wasn't his scream I heard. Too high pitched, too panicky. It must have been my own.

"Where am I?"

"TGH, dear. Best hands in Ontario. You'll be just fine. I'm Donna." She perches on the bedside chair, her green scrubs pulling tight against her ample thighs, the fabric strained. I wonder if my own legs are thatched with scrapes and bruises, thick, oozing scabs. The nurse reaches out, lightly touches my unbandaged hand, and I pull it back reflexively. "Karen," she says, and I wonder quickly how she knows my name, and then it all comes together: my purse in the car. The cab that crashed. Or was crashed into. All the memories past that are hazy, bright blinking hospital lights, doctors and nurses talking at me about anesthesia and surgery.

"How did I get here?" I wonder this one out loud.

"An ambulance. You've been in and out for about a day or so. You had a concussion and surgery for a compound fracture of your ulna. You have an IV, and we've been giving you pain medication, which has knocked you out. We've dialed that back a bit, now. You should feel less groggy. The doctor can tell you about it more when he comes in."

I remember this, the surgery. She takes my hand again. This time, I don't pull away. I look at her face for the first time: a round, happy face, the kind of mouth that smiles even when she's not smiling. I have the opposite. I have perpetual bitch-face. I envy this bubbly nurse in her too-tight scrubs with her bright-pink lips that are lined just a shade too dark and clumpy mascara. She's pretty and not afraid to take my hand. Not nearly as afraid as I am to accept it.

"Honey, I need to call someone for you," she says gently, and I wonder why this is a big issue. "It's been about twenty-four hours. We asked you earlier, and you said to call Scott. He was in your phone. But he didn't pick up, and we haven't heard back."

"Scott is my boyfriend." I realize then, with a sickening swoop, that it's no longer true. "He *was* my boyfriend. He won't pick up for my number."

She clucks, a soft, quick sound filled with too much sympathy. I touch my eyebrow with my good hand just to get it out of her pitying grip.

"You can call my brother. Or my mom," I say, thinking. "Pete or Paula in my phone." Then I remember the issue. A new phone, several months ago, and I've yet to program anyone. I've been dialing by memory. Scott made it in. So did Nikolai. And House of Thai. I flinch at how I must look. They've got to be all tiptoeing around me at the nurses' station, showing each other my contact list and sighing with compassion. *Oh, poor thing.*

I reach over gingerly to pull the rolling tray between the nurse and me, and she scoots back. I grab the pen and TGH letterhead notepad and scribble Pete's number. I rip off the sheet and flutter it in her direction. "This is my brother's number. Call from the nurse's station, not my phone. He might not pick up if he sees my number." Realizing too late that I said the same thing about Scott, I wince. "He's my brother," I explain, as if that makes it better, but I know that looks worse. I'm suddenly too tired to care. A headache pulses behind the bridge of my nose. "I have a broken arm?" I should care more than I do. A broken arm would have devastated me a mere week ago.

"And a few broken ribs. Your ankle has a hairline fracture. We'll get you some more ice and a walking cast, and you'll walk out of here in a few days. The doctor can go through all this with you when he comes in, okay?"

"Okay," I say stupidly and take a deep breath, just to see if I can. Pain slices through my midsection, and I realize the dull throb has been there the whole time.

"I'll get you more pain meds, hon." She pats my good leg and bustles out the door, her pants swooshing as she walks, her rubber soles squeaking on the floor. The door swings behind her, and I wish her back, but nothing happens. A steady, soft beeping comes from the tower of machines next to me. It occurs to me that if I'd stayed semiconscious, who would they have called? Thai takeout? My ex-boyfriend? The question that floats around my brain crystallizes: how long until someone would have noticed I was gone? They would have contacted the police for sure. Then what? Find Paula and Pete? I imagine Pete, a child clinging to each leg, glancing at his ringing phone only to hit decline when he doesn't recognize the number. The truth of that turns my stomach, and I close my eyes.

"Here you go!" Donna comes back in, as cheerily as she left, with a medicine cup of pills and a Styrofoam tumbler of water with a straw. She sets both on the tray and steeples her fingers at me. "You do have a visitor. He claims he doesn't really know you. I've asked him to wait in the hall to make sure you'd want to see him." She cocks her head to the side.

"Who is it?"

"His name is Greg Randolf."

Greg. The very-best-version-of-me Greg. My mouth forms a little O, and I think I say send him in, but I can't be sure. Before I can think, he's standing in the doorway, all tweed coat and big shoulders. He looks like hell.

"Thank God you're okay. I've never... seen anything like that." His voice is hoarse, and his eyes are shot with red, swollen. I wonder if he's slept.

"Hi. Thank you. For coming." I've broken my tongue as well as my arm. I think back through the night, the last things I remember. My lips on his, so soft, and his cheek under my fingertips. I remember his face at the bar when I told him about Paula. He looked at me, not with pity, like Scott and Amy always did, but with compassion. Understanding. He spoke my language. "Sit." I pat the bed next to me and scoot as much as I can, which is about an inch. In his hand is my violin case, the strap dangling loose. He holds it up in my direction before resting it against the wall. He pulls the chair next to my bed.

"You saved my violin," I blurt.

"Interesting… priorities." He laughs softly. His glasses crinkle up on his cheekbones. He rests his hand on mine, an intimate gesture born of fear and courage and something else, the thread between us just like it was in the bar, a zinging current, an electric jolt that leaves my tongue loose and reckless.

"Is this okay?" he asks, and I laugh. "No?" He moves his hand away from mine, and I grab it back, the tips of my fingers grasping at the tips of his.

"I thought you were dead," he says. "When the cops came and they loaded you in that ambulance, there was so much blood…" His voice trails off, and reflexively, I tap the bandage at my forehead and wince in pain.

"Well, the head, I guess. How is the driver? Both drivers, I mean." The back of my throat tastes rancid. "Did they…"

"The cab driver is fine. You took the brunt of the impact. The driver of the other car, he ran a red light. He's in the ICU, has had a few surgeries. Critical condition."

I wonder if he had a family, a child. I wonder if he'll die that way, running a red light, trying to get home from work. I feel irrationally sad in a way that is stupid because the accident was his fault: *he* ran the red light. I try to conjure anger, but I can't. The sadness sits, lumpy and foul in my throat.

Perky Donna is back. "Dear," she singsongs from the doorway. "The police are here. They'd like to talk to Mr. Randolf." Greg jumps back, dropping my hand like it's a hot iron, and he coughs, clears his throat.

"The police? Why?" He wipes a palm on the knee of his khakis.

"Don't look so scared! What, are you a wanted man?" Donna bubbles up. "It's only natural, right?"

"Why natural?" I ask, absently smoothing my blankets down with my good hand, covering my exposed good leg.

"Because Greg here pulled you out of that burning car." She gives us both a wink. "You didn't know? Your boyfriend saved your life."

CHAPTER 4

THE POLICE VISIT IS SHORT. A single detective takes Greg's statement. Greg hands him his license. The cop writes down the information and hands it back. I can barely focus on the conversation. Never mind that my visions swims, a thrumming pulses behind my eyes and around my ears, and it's all I can do not to fall asleep, my heavy head bobbing my chin into my chest.

I'm stunned at Greg's heroics. He pulled me from a car? Turns out, he pulled the cabbie out too. A hero times two. Greg rushes through the description of events, and the officer nods and takes appropriate notes. The car caught on fire under the hood a minute or so after impact. Greg was able to get me out through the passenger-side back door. He pulled the cabbie, who was conscious but pretty shaken up, through the driver's-side door. He thought I was dead, he tells the officer, and when he says this, he looks over at me.

The officer clamps him on the shoulder like an old fraternity brother, an American good ole boy, and then it occurs to me that Greg is American. Hits me like the proverbial ton of bricks. You can tell in his accent, his soft but elongated *oo*'s and *ea*'s. Something slightly Long Island-ish yet less gum snapping than in the movies. He's here on business, and he's surely going home for his lucky underwear. I remember the conversation at the bar. He was here to give a training. For a week? What day is it? I can't ask again; they'd wheel me straight down to neuro. I was in Faraday's on Friday. I was out for about a day. Saturday, possibly Sunday.

The detective asks him about where he lives, and he fumbles and says his license isn't correct. He's moved. He waves his arm around, like it's no big deal, and the detective hands it back. He pockets his wallet, and they talk a bit about the States, California mostly, and I can feel my eyelids drooping. I wonder if Greg is from California, which might as well be another planet. My knowledge of the Golden State comes from Beach Boys songs and *90210* reruns on cable.

The door clicks open, and I hear Greg say, "Thanks," and "good-bye," and my eyelids drift shut of their own volition. I feel my head bob, and I think, although I can't be sure, that Greg kisses my forehead. It might be my imagination. Or a dream. "*I'm glad you're safe.*" The whisper comes to me through that tunnel of half reality between sleeping and waking. Right before I fall off the deep cliff of sleep, I wonder if I'll ever see him again. He has no reason to come back. I'm fine. I can't lie: my heart cracks, just a little.

When I wake up again, it's dark out. The only light in the hospital room comes from above my head, a fluorescent thing that fritzes in and out. My mouth is dry and cottony, and my back aches from sleeping in a half-sitting position. When I move, pain sears up my midsection, and I touch my ribs tenderly. I inspect my sling, a Velcroed contraption that keeps my arm slightly elevated. When I wiggle my fingertips, pain shoots up my forearm and tingles all the way to my shoulder. My bow hand. I curl my fingertips to my thumb. Reflexively, my pinkie arcs up, like a Brit at a tea party, the imaginary bow poised mid-air by the dark-blue canvas sling.

Only the forearm is casted, and I swing my arm in a slow arc, a low, deep G. I could do it. It would be possible. I couldn't be quick. I would be heavy, clunky. I can hear Nikolai now: *lighter touches, my dear.* The whole idea was ridiculous. This break was a real *break.* No more nine a.m. rehearsal. No more Nikolai breathing down my neck, *hit this note harder, longer, don't play* so much *to spec. Take a small solo. Play as a team. Be a leader. Be a team player.* I shift in my bed. My phone has been carefully placed on the nightstand, plugged in to the charger from my purse. I pick it up. No missed calls.

"K-bear! Are you all right?" Pete is hanging in the doorway, lanky as a living clothes hanger.

"Hi, Pete."

He lopes across the room in three long strides and folds himself into the brown pleather visitor's chair. He scoots it back. It was positioned for Greg, and I remember the intimacy of my hand in his. I wish he were there in Pete's place. I wish I hadn't fallen asleep.

"What happened?" Worry creases his forehead.

"What time is it?" I ask, even though I could pick my phone up and look.

"Seven-ish?" Pete grins, almost sheepishly. "I would have come sooner. I got home from racquetball, Mindy told me what happened, and I tried to rush right out, but the kids wanted my attention. You know how it is..." Even though I have no idea how it is, I take it as a personal slight. I think he says these things on purpose.

"What time did the nurse call you?" I ask, dumbly feeling like maybe I should know the answer.

He rubs his left eye. A face touch was always his biggest tell. "I think she left a message with Mindy around three-thirty?" He says this like he's not sure. Even through the Percocet, I realize that four hours is quite a long time to know that your sister is in the hospital and not try to get there.

"Didn't Mindy call you right away?" I ask, incredulous.

"Don't start, please, Karen." He gives me a warning look, and all I can think is, *I'm* in the hospital, and *I'm* not supposed to start? "Tell me what happened? Are you okay? What are your injuries?"

"Two broken ribs, a broken forearm, and a fractured ankle. It could be a lot worse."

"But what *happened*?" Pete asks. "I should have just stayed with you."

I shrug and don't let him off the hook. I don't say, "Don't be silly. It would have happened anyway." He wants me to; I can tell. I let him hang there, suspended by his own guilt, and think, *good.*

"I took a cab home. A car ran a red light," I say, like these things happen. "A man saved my life, pulled me from the car after it caught on fire."

His eyes grow wide as saucers. "What man? It caught on fire?"

"A man I met at Faraday's." A reminder that he should have stayed. This is how we do, Pete and me: a small, circular slow dance with the facade of gentility, all the while throwing well-hidden jabs punctuated by the periodic sharp, stinging uppercut. "Did you call Mom?"

He nods, rubs his chin, and looks toward the door. "I left a message. She didn't pick up."

"Sleeping off last night, I bet." I harrumph out a strangled laugh.

"Kare…" He lets his voice trail off, and I shoot him a glare. He sighs and holds his hands out plaintively. "Give her a break, okay?"

"What about me?" I whine. I know it's a whine, and I wince. I hold up my hand, palm out, to cut him off. I know Pete. A joke was coming, something maybe about a broken arm, whatever. It was my brother's classic role: if a joke can be made, make it. If a responsibility can be ducked or pawned, duck it. But smile big so no one gets mad. Big dimples. I was the only one it didn't work on.

"Aw, Karen. Maybe this is your break. You've been…." He looks around the hospital room, wanly searching for the right words. "Not yourself. Angrier. Distracted. Something. Now you're benched."

"In the championship," I grumble, advancing the sports analogy because it's Pete's language.

"Nah, are you kidding me? This is your rookie year." He means it to be nice. Encouraging.

I bang my good heel against the bed, and it smacks down on a metal rod pushing dangerously close to the mattress's surface, and a sharp throb travels up from my ankle. Awesome. I've injured my good leg.

"What happens to hockey players who get injured in their rookie year?" I challenge.

"Er, not usually anything good." Pete twists his mouth, realizing I've talked him into a trap. Not hard, generally speaking.

I sigh and lean back against my pillows. "Exactly."

When Paula finally blows in, it's with an air of authority she has no right to have. For almost two days, it was nothing but beeps and silence, and then, suddenly, she's here every day with her too-tight-for-her-age jeans and too-strong-for-a-hospital perfume. She's sitting next to my bed, holding my hand when the nurses come in to take my blood pressure or administer pain medication, *tsking* and patting my arm, clucking around the room, pretending to straighten up. She apologizes for being "late" as if we simply had a brunch date and makes an excuse about being out of town for a few days.

"Out of town? In what car?" I ask her. "Where out of town?"

I can't tell if I'm pinning her down out of a true concern. After all, her car rambles along with more than two hundred thousand miles, and her cell phone is perpetually lost. I often think that Paula could just wander off the face of the earth, and who would know? Who, besides Pete and I, would care? I think, mostly, I'm trying to catch her in her lie, but she's always slippery, and even if I did, I'm not sure she'd care. She's been here for two days in a row, and it feels like a year.

"How is the pain?" She changes the subject, her brows knitted in concern that could be real.

"I'm fine, Mom. I'm going home tomorrow, anyway." I've been here four days, and my concussion is better, and my ankle is healing. I hobble around on a walking cast to and from the bathroom. My arm has been set and air-casted, and I'm impatient with the nurses and doctors, confined to one room with a growing stack of gossip magazines that Paula brings me next to the bed. I've never read celebrity magazines in my life. I can't imagine who cares about this stuff. But I'm bored, and the glossy pages beg to be flicked through.

Abbie, the day nurse, watches us out of the corner of her eye, and I'd love to know what she makes of Paula. My mother's blond hair is curled around her heavily made-up face as though she goes right from here to a club, which probably isn't far from the truth. Her cleavage is lined with folds of loose skin, and she wears a slinky turquoise see-through top tucked into low-slung jeans with a wide, flashy belt. High-heeled boots tap the bedframe, an irritating *ding, ding, ding* that reverberates through the mattress and buzzes my ankle.

"Did you bring my clothes?" I ask her. I'd asked her yesterday to please bring me wide-leg black yoga pants that I could fit around my walking cast, a few tank tops, and a sweatshirt. The temperature in the hospital swings from the upper eighties back down to the sixties in a matter of hours, and it seems like, no matter what, I'm perpetually uncomfortable.

She swings a grocery bag onto the bed from the floor, and it lands with a thump an inch from my bad leg. I inhale sharply and shoot her a look. I open it with my good hand. It contains a pair of black leggings and a few haphazard T-shirts, one of which I don't even recognize.

"Mom. This isn't what I asked for." I huff, and Abbie busies herself with the tower of monitors next to my bed.

"Sure it is. You said black pants and a T-shirt. I brought you what I could find." Paula bends over and pulls a bottle of lime-green nail polish out of her purse. I watch her uncap it, touch up her index fingernail, and blow on it. She splays her hand in front of my face. "Am I too old for this color?"

"Mom." My voice is sharp, but I can't help it. I have so little control in this room. I don't control when I sleep or what the temperature is. I can't get my own water or my food. If I want a snack, I have to buzz someone and wait a half hour. Without the right clothes, I'm resigned to wearing a thin, freezing-cold hospital gown. I can't ask this of Pete. I'm stuck with Paula and her hopeless incompetence. I hold up the leggings. "Do these look like they will go over a walking cast? And what is this T-shirt?"

She sits up and grins proudly. "It's one of mine!" She shrugs. "It might not fit you. You've always been so broad across the shoulders." I must make a face because she giggles, a high-pitched childlike gurgle, and she waves her hand around. Her rings and bracelets jingle together. "Oh, don't look like that. It's not a bad thing."

"But I wanted tank tops. And sweatshirts. Layers I can take on and off."

"You know, you should let me paint your toenails now that you can't wear shoes." She stands up and fishes around in her purse, producing a bottle of blue glitter polish. She positions herself at the end of the bed before I can stop her. She plops her purse on the mattress, and from the corner pocket of her bag glints a flash of metal. A flask? I poke it with my good toe. "A little color never hurt anyone." She *tsks* at me, shaking her head.

"Mom. Paula. You're not listening to me. I don't want my toenails painted. I want to be comfortable, here in this room." My voice is rising to a panicky pitch, and yes, that's definitely a flask. The woman brought a flask. To a hospital. "I don't know why this is too much to ask of you. Black pants. Tank tops. A sweatshirt jacket. Why is what *I want* never ever enough? Why—"

Dr. Patel, my orthopedist, interrupts my rising tirade with his brisk entrance. The door *whooshes* shut behind him. "Hello! How is everyone feeling today?" He ignores, or perhaps just doesn't notice, my welling tears, my impending meltdown. He takes in Paula with a swift glance, and I watch her go from clucking hen to purring cat, narrow-eyed seductress in a matter of seconds.

"You must be Karen's doctor." She offers her hand, leaning in and all but petting him, her décolletage on display. She takes in his smooth brown skin, his dignified, graying hair and dazzling smile, and her eyes flick to his hand, noting the absence of a wedding ring. She calculates it all, right there in front of me, the way I've seen her do a hundred times. Teachers, doctors, dentists, my whole childhood. Every man was a possibility. Parent–teacher conferences were potential dates. Teeth cleanings were meet-cutes.

"No. No, no, no." I struggle to sit up, pulling

my casted leg with me, and my voice vibrates off the stark white walls. "No. Paula, *shut up*. Just get out!" I can feel the unreasonableness, that bleak empty feeling in my gut that says there's no way to come back from this, no way to recapture dignity. I can tell in the shocked look on Dr. Patel's face, Abbie's dropped jaw, the way Paula hisses at me, "Karen, what is wrong with you?"

But it's too late, and the blood is pumping through my arms and legs, the heat climbing up my neck and pulsing in my head. "Just get out! *Now!*" I scream it much too loud and angrier than the situation warrants, and even as I know this, I can't stop. I point toward the door. Everyone stares at me in shock, their heads bopping back and forth between Paula and me. There is one pregnant second where all I hear is the *beep, beep, beep* of the heart monitor and Paula's raspy breathing, coming in short, panicked breaths, before she picks up her purse and pulls it up on her shoulder, slowly like she's underwater. She doesn't look at me or make excuses. She doesn't speak at all.

She simply leaves.

The rain patters against the sidewalk and my face as I wait. I'm tucked under the awning outside the hospital doors. Every time someone walks past in the hallway inside, they slow down just enough for the doors to swoosh open and shut.

"I can't call your mother for you?" Abbie's been

like this since my meltdown yesterday. Asking me a million different ways if she can call Paula. Reminding me that I only have one mother. How do you fit your whole life into an explanation without sounding defensive? What do I have to defend myself for? I don't. I crane my neck and look up and down the street, looking for the cab, just for something to do.

"No. I'm fine. Thank you, Abbie. For everything." I give her an encouraging smile. A don't-feel-sorry-for-me-I'm-just-fine smile.

"Your brother?"

"Nope, really." I pat her shoulder. "I called a cab. It's not a big deal. I promise, okay? My apartment is about five blocks from here. I'd walk if it weren't for…" I wave toward my foot and shrug. "Please. I'm okay." I have nothing but my purse, my violin with its rigged and tied strap slung over my good arm, and a plastic bag with my mother's T-shirt. I'm wearing the dreaded leggings, the left one pushed up to my knee, slowly pinching off the circulation. My right arm hangs, a heavy albatross around my neck. Abbie pulls her windbreaker around her, making no move to leave.

A small, late-model Honda pulls up to the curb. The passenger-side window rolls down, and Greg leans over.

"Need a lift?" he asks with a wide grin.

I shoot Abbie a look. She shakes her head, palms

out. "This was not me. I would have let you take a cab."

I limp to the car. "How did you know I was here?" I ask him suspiciously. He laughs.

"I didn't. I called the hospital to see if you were out, and they said you were leaving today but that I'd better hurry down because you were on your way out. When I got to the parking lot, there you were." He jumps out of the car and jogs around to the passenger side. "Do you really need a ride? Who is coming for you?"

"I called a cab. I'm fine, really."

"Are you always so obstinate? Besides, calling a cab worked out so well last time." He opens the passenger-side door and helps me in. His hand feels warm despite the cold rain. The heat in the car is blasting. I'm shivering. Out the window, I wave to Abbie, who dubiously waves back. I give her an impish smile. My ankle aches, and I just want to be home. Tea and a cookie. Oh, crap, I remember that I have no food in my apartment. I look at my ankle and my arm. How am I going to do this—this living alone with only half of a useful body thing? I quell the rising panic.

I text Pete. *Is there any way you could go to the store for me?*

Greg glances over at me, and when we make eye contact, he smiles. Now that we're alone in the car and I'm lucid, the silence feels awkward. He clears his throat. "Where to?"

"Oh, um… make a left out of the parking lot."

He drives carefully. Slow and steady as though he has a lemon meringue pie on the passenger's seat. I bite back a smile. I eye the other cars only a bit nervously. I wondered if I'd have a fear of riding in cars. I'd read about that once, but Greg's driving is so slow, so smooth, that I settle back, more content than anxious for the first time in days. Except for my periodic turn instructions, the car is silent. I yawn. The radio plays classic rock on low volume, and the interior is spotless. It's a rental.

"Where do you live?" I blurt out, remembering the conversation between him and the detective a few days ago.

"New Jersey. But the company I work for is talking about transferring me, so I don't know where I'll end up. I grew up in Syracuse and lived there for a long time."

"The company you train people for." I remember his "worst day" story the night at Faraday's, which feels like a million years ago. "Are you still here or here again?"

He doesn't answer right away, and he taps the steering wheel in a little rhythm along with the song. "Here again. I flew home and came back." His words are short and clipped, and I wonder if this ride has irritated him. Is it not what he signed up for? I remember his words, "*I'm glad you're safe,*" and I think maybe I made them up. I remember the way his mouth felt against mine that night of the accident. Even though I'd kissed him, he'd kissed back, right? *Right?* I remember his hand holding mine in the hospital bed.

So why is it now, my heart hammers a hundred gallops an hour, and he sits there, like a chilled cool cucumber or worse, like he's doing this out of pity? I should have taken the cab. I shift in my seat. Every movement feels huge and clunky, and I have no idea where to put my good hand.

At my apartment, Greg rushes out of the car to help me up the steps. As we stand in front of my apartment door, I'm self-conscious of my space. My apartment has always been more utilitarian than aesthetic. My free time is spent practicing or on the road, focused on the next concert, the next piece. I don't so much *live* there as I *reside* there.

I take a deep breath and push open the door. Despite my mental preparation, I've forgotten how stark it actually is—no pictures of family and friends on end tables. In fact, no end tables. A sofa, an entertainment center with a fifteen-year-old, rarely used television. Bare walls. Not even a welcome mat. Some Walmart-acquired pots and pans. A pine table and chairs in the kitchen. If it weren't for the music stand and sheet music on every flat surface, not to mention the pervading scent of rosin, it would look like a hotel room.

"Did you just move in?"

"Nope," I grunt as I flop onto the couch. "Been here about six years." I offer no explanation, suddenly, inexplicably offended by his inquiries. I hear him in the kitchen, opening cupboards and the refrigerator. He appears again in the doorway.

"You have literally nothing. Like, I found teabags. But no food. Not even stale bread. How is this possible?" Dimples. His glasses glint in the light.

"I'm a minimalist." I smirk at him, and he laughs. The truth is more that I'm busy. Or lazy. And I eat on the go often. I've had no reason to eat at home. Why stock food? I'm never here. I think of Scott and our midnight jazz bar dates or mornings at the coffee shop.

"Okay, here." He hands me a pen and paper. I give him a blank look. "Make a list. I can't leave you like this. You'll starve to death, apparently, before you ask for help."

Shaking his head, he walks back into the kitchen. I hear banging and the water running. I think about a list, all the normal things. *Bread, milk, eggs, butter.* I wonder if I can put Hobnobs on there like I'm some kind of senior citizen. I skip the fizzy raspberry club soda and just put plain club soda because isn't that more sophisticated? Then again, he might drop everything off, and then we'll shake hands and go our separate ways, and I'll be stuck with terrible plain club soda for the next six weeks. *Six weeks!* What am I going to do for six weeks? In this apartment.

"Ahem." Greg, hovering over me, clears his throat, and when I look up, he's holding a mug of tea and three cookies. Three cookies!

"Where did you find those?" The level of relief I feel is unwarranted.

"In the cabinet. As far as I could tell, not eaten by mice."

I take the tea from his hands. "By any chance, would you want to get me the—"

"Honey?" He smiles again. "I added it. You had no sugar, but you had honey. I took a chance. You don't seem to… have things you don't use."

We stay this way for a full-on minute, him standing above me, me staring up at him, my rescue hero with tea and cookies and a grocery list. I look away, embarrassed by the tears stinging my eyes. It's pathetic that this simple act of caring could possibly make me cry, even a little. This is what people do for each other. This is humanity. Kindness.

He leaves then, with the list and a little salute. I must doze, because the next thing I know, he's back, banging through the front door, his arms filled with bags, more than I've asked him to buy. I hear him in the kitchen, putting everything away, and he brings me a sandwich, setting it down carefully on the arm of the chair.

"So there're these great things called coffee tables. You can put stuff on them? Some people even put books there."

I laugh and gesture at the floor, where I've set my mug. He perches on the edge of the sofa, and I hike up sideways between him and the back cushions, propped up on my sore ankle. It throbs, but I don't care. He's kept me at arm's length all day, and it's driving me crazy.

"Will you be okay here? Who will you call?" He asks this like he's not coming back, and my stomach bottoms out.

"My brother is around. My mom is… around. I'll be fine." I force a smile. I reach out with my good arm and cover his hand. His head jerks up like I've burned him, and he clears his throat.

"Thank you. Really. I don't know what I would have done today." I say this sincerely. His wrists are thick, with the lightest of downy hair covering his arms and the tops of his hands. He has large, wide fingers and neatly trimmed nails. He's too broad for the space he's trying to occupy, and he shifts uncomfortably. The heat from his back travels through my walking cast, and my skin buzzes.

I sit up to hug him, a thank-you for all he's done. He holds me back. He smells like clean air and pine and shower soap. I know so little about him. He's barely said a word about himself. I don't know when he has to leave or if he'll be back. Will he go back to New Jersey? Will he be transferred?

"Will you come back?" I ask, a needy high school kind of girl.

"I'll check in on you," he whispers. He pulls away and clears his throat and gives my good shoulder a soft, playful punch. "What would happen to you if I didn't?"

I kiss his cheek, and he turns his head, just for a

second. The kiss lands shy of his mouth, and I feel his breath against my cheek. Neither of us moves. We breathe. I could lean over and just kiss his mouth, blame it on the Percocet, the way I blamed the first kiss on the alcohol. Under my hand, his bicep flexes twice.

Then he's up and across the room. He stands at the door, his back to me, and doesn't turn around. "I got your number from your phone. I'll call you, okay?"

I nod. The door clicks shut before I can respond.

CHAPTER 5

A WEEK PASSES. AMY TEXTS ME half-heartedly with a *glad you're ok. I'll come visit!* But no follow-up as to when. Nikolai sends a generic *hope you're doing well* email. I ignore both.

Pete visits twice, bringing milk, coffee, and knock-knock jokes—typical Pete with his uncanny sense of what's just enough to get him off the hook. He keeps telling me he'll bring the kids by. I genuinely miss my nieces and nephews, but then I picture Mindy here—she's never been—standing in the middle of the room, eyeing the furniture warily, noting the lack of personality. She thinks there's something wrong with me. She told Pete years ago. I was too driven. I was too cold. I was too mechanical. When Pete told me that and I asked him what he said back to her, he just shrugged. "What could I say, Kar? You aren't nice to her, either." Either way, my apartment would confirm it.

I don't hear from Paula at all. Despite my irritation, I ask Pete to check in on her.

"Why? She's fine." Pete has his long legs stretched out in front of him, and he's folded into the sofa, encroaching on my space. He flicks through my DVR. "What have you been watching? Home improvement shows? The *Real Housewives*?"

"A girl's DVR should be allowed to be private." I shoot him a look and yank the remote out of his hand. "Check on Mom, okay? She doesn't avoid me like this. Who knows if she's face down in a gutter somewhere?"

"Karen, she is not *that* bad. You're so dramatic. You should have gone into theater instead of music." Pete just laughs. "So what will you do now? Are you okay, money wise?" He pulls off his baseball hat, smoothes his hair, and replaces the cap.

"I'm fine. I have a little money saved. Eventually, I have to go see about disability. I know I'm eligible. I think." The whole idea of going back, to the concert hall, to Nikolai, turns my stomach. When I first got home, the orchestra sent flowers. I don't know who initiated it, but the arrangement sat, wilting, on the kitchen table, surrounded by a ring of curling, crispy leaves. Sprays of vibrant lilies shaped like fluted horns in a vase so big I couldn't carry it myself. The water level hovered near the bottom, grayish-green.

My phone chirps, an incoming text, and I snatch it up and mumble, "Speak of the devil." But I blink at the display. It's not Paula. It's from an unknown phone number.

How are you feeling?

I pause for a moment then type back, *I've had better months, but okay. Who is this?*

Within seconds: *Oh, sorry. It's Greg. I said I'd check up on you. :)*

My heart picks up an irrational speed. *Oh, then in that case, I'm out of Hobnobs, and I need raspberry pop. Come back?*

Immediately, *I'll be back next week. Can you wait that long?*

I'm in dire need of cookies.

What are Hobnobs anyway?

Pfffft Americans.

I wait, but he doesn't text back. Pete's engrossed in *The Bachelor*, and he taps me with his toe. "Who's your friend?" He nods to the phone.

I shake my head with a small smile. "No one you know."

It must be the boredom. The walls of my apartment are closing in on me. I can't watch another television show or movie, and when I try to read a book, my mind wanders to Greg.

I've been alone for three whole days, hobbling around, eating jam sandwiches and ketchup potato chips. Paula doesn't call. Pete texts once a day with the same text, *How are you feeling?* and I type back, *Better today!* but I'm not better today. I'm actually looking forward to my doctor appointment at the end of the week.

I attempt to play, the violin balanced feebly against my shoulder, my chin on the chinrest. But I can't manage the finger positions with my cast. Frustrated, I set my violin back in the case. I dust off the television stand. Months-old rosin dust has settled on everything, and for once, I've spent enough time in the living room to notice. Dusting all flat surfaces takes me about fifteen minutes. There aren't that many. In my bedroom, I wander around.

I should miss playing more than I do. I should be panicking at the thought of never playing again. I should be dramatically missing the lost hours, forgetting pieces I worked so hard to memorize. Instead, I feel guilt that I have none of these feelings. Out of habit, I still run through pieces as I fall asleep at night, trying half-heartedly to keep the memorization sharp. Mostly, I've replaced my musical obsession with apathy.

In the back of my closet, I dig out a plastic bag filled with yarn and knitting needles. When I was a girl, when Paula and Dad were still married and happy, I remember sitting on her lap, watching those two needles wrap around each other so fast they looked like one. The metal of the sticks, and Paula's nails and her rings, made a kind of beautiful, rhythmic music. I'd hold that neat, tight little ball of yarn. "*Wind that up for me, Kar-bear.*" I'd fall asleep there to the clacking of her knitting, blanket after useless blanket, to the backdrop of *Jeopardy!* and the tinkling of ice in a whiskey tumbler. As the years faded and I grew too large for her lap, the blankets turned into scarves, and the lulling voice of Alex Trebek muted to silence.

Then there was a fight, or a series of them, but in my mind they've melded into one culminating argument. In my memory, Paula was knitting, Dad was yelling, and I hovered in the hallway, hunkered down against the stair rail. They yelled together, their voices climbing over each other until the crash. I ran in. Paula sat there in her chair, those needles and yarn in her lap, covered in ice and liquor, her hands ever moving to the internal rhythm in her head. The *clakety-clack* of needles and nails and rings never slowed. She just kept right on with that blanket, a yellow and green chevron-stripe afghan, like she wasn't soaking wet and stinking. The next day, Dad was gone, and the yarn sat, unraveled and disheveled in the basket next to the chair, collecting puffs of dust on the sticky, drying threads. I never saw her pick it up again until she handed me a bag of all her old yarn and needles, and I shoved it in the back of my closet.

So now, I hold this old plastic bag filled with fifteen-year-old yarn and wonder if I could do it. Clearly Paula replaced knitting with drinking, but everyone needs a hobby. I look at my dead arm, pinned flat against my midsection with a sling, and wiggle my fingers. Knitting isn't an option. In the bottom of the bag lies a crochet hook. I pull out the yarn, a pretty bright blue, almost a turquoise.

I YouTube crocheting instructions. A slipknot, a

single stitch. One hand stays relatively stationary. I give it a whirl. My fingers are numb and clumsy, but it's doable. And more importantly, it's something to do. So I stitch one long chain, almost as long as my leg. It takes me several hours, but I'm focused, and when I finally look up, like in a fugue, it's after eleven.

But look at it! It's beautiful. I pick up my phone and snap a picture of it. I want to show someone how useful I am, but disgustedly, I realize there's no one to call. I hesitate only a second before I attach the picture to a text message and press "send."

I wait. Five minutes later, Greg texts back. *You made that? With a broken arm? That's kind of amazing.*

I know! I'm bored out of my mind. Come back!

I wait, but he doesn't text back. I'm about to give up when my phone rings.

"Hello?"

"You must be bored if you want me back. Either that or you need groceries."

"Both, actually."

He sighs into a pregnant pause. "When I come back, I'll bring you tea. And cookies, okay?"

"Really? I'd love that."

"Yep, you are officially going stir crazy."

He laughs, and maybe I should feel defensive at my lack of company, but I don't. I want to hand him every part of me, this man I barely know. I don't want to be coy. I don't want to play games or tease him. I just want him to know, somehow, that I've spent the majority of today, and if I'm honest, the past six days, thinking about him. I want him to instantly know me.

"Actually, you're the first person whose company I've truly enjoyed in a very long time." I take a deep breath as I say it, knowing it sounds a bit pathetic and needy. When he doesn't answer right away, I rush on. "I have Paula. I have Pete. I guess I have Amy, if I wanted. I should really call her. I used to have Scott."

"Who's Scott?"

"My ex. He broke up with me the night before I met you."

"Did you love him?" His reply is immediate. Interested. Curious.

I pause, partly because it's an extraordinarily intimate question, and partly because I don't immediately know the answer. Greg's voice, low and soft, almost whispering, and the time of night give the sensation of being in a cocoon.

"I guess I thought I did, but I haven't given him much thought in the past week, so maybe not." I pause. "I don't think I loved him in any exceptional way. I loved him because he was there, and he was easy. And I was already tied to him through music. I loved him in a convenient way. We were compatible, never fought." I stop and think before I realize that's all of it. I think of how in movies, the hero always lists *the way your socks never match* or *the way you use half a box of floss a day* as reasons to love someone. I never had those with Scott. I didn't know all his quirks, and they certainly never felt like tender points, rom-com reasons for loving someone. He had a tendency to chew with his mouth open and hold a napkin up to his mouth so he could talk at the same time. I always thought he was gross and simultaneously efficient.

"I think if you can list all the reasons you love someone, then maybe it isn't real?" Greg says.

"What do you mean?"

"Like maybe when you truly love someone, it defies convenience and rationale. Like maybe if you have to fight hard for it, it's somehow truer. You're not together because you can be. You're together because you really want to be." He's talking so softly that I can barely hear him.

"Have you been in love?"

He coughs into the phone. "Not recently."

I wonder if he's drunk or what he's really saying. I wonder how we keep ending up in these intense conversations.

"Isn't it better, though, to pursue a relationship with someone that's at least available to you?" I laugh to lighten it up, but he doesn't laugh back. I take a chance. "Than, say, with someone in another country?"

Shameless flirting. I stretch out on the sofa on my good side and pull a pillow against my chest.

"I'm sure there are charmingly available Canadian

men." I can hear the hesitation in his voice, as though he doesn't exactly want to flirt back, but he doesn't *not* want to either. I decide to push.

"Yeah, but none of them have saved my life."

Then, thankfully, he finally laughs.

CHAPTER 6

REG CALLS ME—NEVER THE OTHER way around. I text once in a while when I'm bored with reading or crocheting or watching realtor shows. But if I ever call him, it rings once and goes straight to voicemail, like he hits decline. Fast. He always texts back, *sorry in a meeting! Call you tonight!* Unlike other men, he actually does.

"Have you called your mom?" he presses one night, his voice in that late-night, low rumble that I feel in my legs and my toes. "You have one mother. Call her."

Sigh. "I know. But you don't understand. She's a train wreck, and I don't feel like I have room right now for two of those."

"I do understand. What if you just called her and said hi. Like nothing happened?" He's chewing something. An apple. A cracker.

"What are you eating?" I pretend to be irritated.

"Hobnobs. Call your mother."

I've thought about it, truly I have. The thing is,

Paula lives in that space between knowing there's a problem and addressing it. She counts on her own volatility to keep people from calling her out on her shit. It works on Pete. It used to work on my dad. To be honest, it generally works on me. I don't have the energy for her. I dial her number. No answer. I leave a message, surprising myself. If we're being honest, I do it so I can tell Greg later.

I text him: *I called her. What do I win?*

I wait, the phone in hand, for five full minutes.

My undying admiration. Good enough.

Me: coffee or tea?

Him: Coffee. Tea? What is this, Britain?

Me: Hey. I'm a tea kind of girl.

Him: You're something.

Me: Books or movies?

Him: Movies based on books.

Me: That's totally the wrong answer.

Him: Board games or video games?

Me: Board games. I'm too old for video games.

Him: How old are you anyway?

Me: You never ask a lady her age. How old are you?

Him: God, you're sexist.

Me: I thought you said sexy.

No reply.

Me: When do you come back?

Him: Soon. I hope.
Me: Not soon enough.

"What are you doing this weekend?" If it was the eighties, I'd have the phone cord twirled around my ankle, and I'd snap gum in his ear.

He sighs. "A family reunion. I don't want to go. Should I skip it? Drive to Canada?"

"Yes. This is what I'm suggesting! Tell me about your family."

"Oh." He hesitates. "Not much to tell. I'm not close with any of them. Just a bunch of elderly aunts." He laughs. "But I'm coming back next week. Is that soon enough?"

"Barely. But yes."

I sigh.

"Dinner?" I ask hopefully.

He's silent for a beat. "Yes. Definitely dinner."

I officially have a date. When we hang up, I wish I could tell someone.

I change my outfit seven hundred times like I'm sixteen. I settle on dark wide-leg jeans, a deep-V shirt, and one silly black kitten heel. The other foot is still encased in a clunky walking cast. Silver jewelry, earrings that swing. Light makeup. It's one of those nights where everything just works. All the flyaways that I typically have to wrangle into place with a dryer sheet just behave.

God, I'm so nervous. I haven't been on a first date in at least four years. I remember that first night with Scott, the furtive slip of his phone number against all convention while our respective dates waited in the food tent. I remember the way my heart raced so much I thought it would fly out of my chest. That was nothing compared to this.

I can't eat. My good foot taps and patters against the tile kitchen floor, waiting. He texts me, *Be there in five!* I like how there are no games with Greg. He says he'll call, and he calls. He says he'll be there in five, and he'll be here. He's such an adult. Scott used to make plans and show up two hours late, dinner reservations be damned. He blamed it on his adult ADD, his inability to focus. He was distracted by the muse or scatting in his living room.

When the doorbell rings, I buzz him upstairs and wait. He knocks softly a shave-and-a-haircut tap, and I laugh to myself. By the time I open the door, I'm almost breathless from anticipation, and my stomach rolls with nerves.

Greg looks the way I remember. When he smiles, he's all dimples and sparkling eyes, and I'm irritated with how crazy about him I am. It's so unlike me. I like men *well enough* but never like this.

He takes a deep breath. "You look... great."

"I would twirl but..." I point to my foot. He

laughs. It's deeply resonant and sounds better in person than it does on the phone. Or text.

We stand there, he in the hallway, me in the doorway, smiling at each other, and I realize that without a doubt he's as crazy about me as I am about him. There's a certain freedom in that—to be exactly myself. I can like jazz or not. I can like regular fizzy pop or raspberry. I can chew gum for two minutes and throw it away if I want.

I realize he has one hand behind his back.

I raise my eyebrows. "Whatcha got there?"

He brings his arm around, and in his hand is a small, blue, familiar container.

"Chocolate Hobnobs!" I clap. I'd jump up and down if I could.

He laughs. "Better than flowers?"

I place them carefully on the kitchen table, and when I look back up, his face is flushed, and his eyes crinkle at the corners.

I kiss his cheek. "Definitely."

At dinner, our feet touch under the table. Our hands brush when he fills my water glass. I giggle in ways I don't generally giggle at men. I'm both enamored and, from a bird's-eye view, a tad disgusted with myself.

"Tell me about your mom." I've had just enough alcohol for the question to be excusable.

He sighs and leans back against his chair. "Why? We were having so much fun without that." But he's smiling in a way that means he won't really mind telling me.

"Because it helps me. My mother is… she's never been a mother. That's not true. She used to be. When I was little. She'd come to performances, do my hair, watch me with bated breath." And pursed lips at every small timing error, but I don't say that part.

He twiddles a fork between the fingers of his right hand. "My mother was sick. Schizophrenic, I'm pretty sure. Completely undiagnosed. I had no idea until I was in high school. I read an article in the newspaper about schizophrenia, and something clicked. I just knew. So I went to the library, in the days before the Internet, and looked up the DSM. I got chills. It was uncanny. She used to rant all the time. She was forced to drop out of college because her professors stole her research. The bank was stealing her money. We had to stay indoors. I was isolated, mostly friendless."

"I'm sorry. I had no idea." I open and close my mouth, unsure what else to say.

He shrugs. "It was a long time ago. I wish she had known she was ill, so we could get help. My father wasn't in the picture. Either I never met him or he left before I remember, I suspect because she was sick. I asked her, but she'd rage. He was 'part of it,' she said. I didn't know what that meant, but I knew enough not to ask."

"How horrible. Did you have any support? Grandparents?"

He nodded. "I did. My grandmother was around, and don't get me wrong, Mom was surprisingly competent. I wasn't eating Cheetos for dinner. I just had… different rules than everyone else."

He finally looks up, meets my eyes, and smiles. "I've never told anyone that before. Isn't that weird?"

"Really? Why?" I reach out and slide my hand over his. It feels so natural. He stares at it for a minute then turns his hand over, and we sit like that, palm to palm. I stare at his hands and think about them in my hair, on my body. Large, square, neatly trimmed nails. I lace my fingers through his, he lets me, and I can scarcely breathe.

He stares at our entwined hands. "It always felt like a violation somehow. Once I realized she was sick, I did anything I could to help her. Then she died and…"

"You felt like you had to make it up to her?" I supply, thinking of Paula and all our missed opportunities. How would I feel if she was suddenly gone, leaving me unable to fix it?

"Yeah," he says softly. "Like that. Plus, she left me money, and I was, for a very long time, exceedingly angry. I've been dealing with it, in my own way, for the past decade. I never knew she had so much money. She inherited it from an uncle. I… never knew. She was too paranoid to use it, I think."

"Why were you angry?"

"Because we used to ration heat. She acted like we were two steps away from homeless. She hoarded money the way some people hoard cats or newspapers."

"Have you talked to anyone about it? Like a therapist?" I turn his hand over and run my thumb up the center of his palm.

He takes a sharp breath. "Just you. Just now."

"I'm sorry," I say softly. "And I can relate, at least a little."

"I know." He smiles. "That's why this is easy."

He walks me to my apartment door, holding hands. At my door, he falters, like a teenager after a dance. "Wait. I feel like I need to tell you something." He steps away, putting cold air between us, and I reach out, panicky, to pull him back.

"Just," I start, and he looks away. "Just don't. Come in. Please? No worries tonight. I've just had the best time. I've needed this." I step toward him, closing the gap. It occurs to me that he might have a girlfriend back in the States. I open my mouth to ask and close it. I look up and down the hallway. I want to know but not.

"Ah, I should go." But he doesn't move. He leans toward me.

"Come in." I tug gently on his coat. He sways forward, resting his forehead against mine, and we wait there, for the kiss I know is going to happen.

When I kiss him, his mouth is warm and soft and responsive, just the way I remember it, and I thread my fingers up through his hair. His mouth moves under mine, his tongue seeking me out. I pull away and hold his hand with my good hand, lead him into the apartment, and bump the door shut with my hip.

Standing in my living room, he looks around as if he's never been here before. I kiss him again, and this time, there's no hesitation. No *wait, I should tell you*—just a hungry want. His hands find my waist, slide down my hips, and my sling hangs between us, cumbersome and awkward.

He laughs softly. "I don't want to hurt you."

I tug him back to me, my good arm wrapped around his neck. "Shut up." I kiss his face, his neck, the soft fold behind his ear. I feel his breath against my cheek, quick and light, and he pushes me back against the door.

"To the bedroom?" I whisper against his neck. *Please say yes.*

He hesitates, and for a moment I'm sure he's going to say no. He goes that still. His hands pause, his mouth unmoving next to my cheek. I slide out from between him and the metal door and guide his hand behind me. I lead him to the bedroom, and he follows.

I kneel on the bed, cradling his chin in my hands. "Okay?"

He doesn't answer. Instead, he kisses me, crushing

me against him, a hungry growl against my mouth. When he eases me back against the bed, I forget that he hesitated. I forget that he was unsure because he now seems nothing *but* sure. I forget about anything else in my life: Paula, Amy, the TSO, my injuries. The only thing that exists is Greg, his hands on my body, his mouth on mine, and the way he makes me feel as though I'm the most important person in his life. I could get used to this.

In the morning, he's wrapped around me, coiled in the quilt, pillows tossed haphazardly around the room.

I sit up. "What happened here?" I laugh.

He looks around and pulls me back down to the bed, into the cocoon of blankets. "Who cares?" he mumbles against my bare shoulder.

I turn on my side, and he lies behind me, his mouth hot against my spine. His breathing levels as if he's fallen back to sleep. I have nowhere to go. It's seven a.m., and I hunker down, burrowing myself against the wall of his chest. "Do you have a girlfriend?" I ask quietly, and I feel his breath against the skin of my back.

"No." He kisses my neck. "Why did you ask?"

"I don't know. You seem unsure about this, that's all. It's a little weird. Most guys are thrilled to get in bed with a girl. I had to drag you here."

He lightly nudges my back with his elbow and

laughs. "Oh, that's a bit dramatic. You did not. I was pretty willing."

"Eventually…"

He sighs. "Well, I'm traveling for work. I didn't want a one-night stand. Plus, it's been a long time since I've done… this."

I laugh and kiss his hand. "Well, you were pretty good at it."

He pulls me against him but says nothing. We lie there, breathing together for a few minutes. Finally, he says, "If I had to go away on business, would you be able to come? Would you want to come?"

"Yes! Seriously? I'd love to. I'm so bored." I stare straight ahead, holding my breath, and trace his hands with my nails. "Where?"

"California."

"I've never been." Sun, sand, palm trees. "Careful now. I could fall in love with you." I whisper this part. He's quiet for so long I wonder if he even heard me.

He kisses the back of my head. "I know," he whispers back.

CHAPTER 7

W HEN I WAS FOURTEEN, PAULA took me
to Fairmont Le Chateau Frontenac in
Quebec. I'd stared at those steep peaks
and that sparkling green roof and knew I'd never stay
anywhere nicer than that. I'd run my feet between
the two-thousand-thread-count sheets and the heavy
brocade blankets and stared out at the St. Lawrence
River from our window table from Champlain. I
picked at my *foie gras*. I listened to Paula ramble on
about rehearsal schedules and audition times. The
heavy reality, known even then, was that my life had
already peaked. I didn't realize what the next few
years would bring, that my father would leave one
night so early in the morning the trains weren't even
running yet, or that Paula would not just slip into
her brandy like most middle-aged unemployable
housewives but that she'd fall headfirst into it,
dragging Pete and me with her. But I already sensed
that somehow, I'd look back on that moment from
some distant future with remorse that I hadn't fully
appreciated it.

With Paula, my memory of our trip is one of

isolation. She networked with other stage parents, and we attended black-tie parties meant more for the adults than the students. I remember boredom. I remember trying futilely to connect with other students and feeling excluded, not so much that I'd been turned away or rebuffed but isolated in that I seemed to be the only teenager there interested in connection in the first place. Their waxy, placid faces expressionless as they perched on the velvet chairs. Their thin, polite smiles and watchful eyes. The understanding that this mattered less to me than perhaps anyone in the room. By virtue of that alone, I was cast out.

The Grand Del Mar resembles the Chateau Frontenac in level of luxury only. The Spanish-style stucco and red clay roof are a stark contrast to the Renaissance style of the Frontenac, but the interior is just as decadent with its sweeping staircases and dark, marble-inlaid flooring. With its wide, expansive lobby and its leafy palm plants and Greg, warmth tingles from my toes to the top of my head.

"Greg," I hiss as a concierge takes our bags. "This is crazy. Can you afford this?"

"It's on the company." He quickly pockets his credit card and picks lint off his sleeve. "Just relax. Enjoy it."

He shifts on his feet, ill at ease and looking around. Maybe he's wondering what he's gotten himself into. A luxury hotel. A somewhat mobile invalid. He wanders away from me to the far end of the lobby and gazes out at the rolling hills of a pristine golf course. I absently pick up a pamphlet and thumb through it.

"You know," I say thoughtfully, coming up behind him. "This hotel is famous for its golf course. Do you?"

"Do I golf?" He laughs, but it's strangled and a tiny bit hollow. He turns to me. "No. I have but not in years, and I wasn't any good." I may be imagining a wistful edge. "And then I sort of ran out of time."

"Isn't that a pre-req for a corporate man? Must use appropriate buzzwords like *synergistic* and *mindshare*, must own"—I tilt my head and eye him head to toe with a sideways smile. I take the cotton collar of his shirt between my fingertips—"polo shirts in all colors, including pink, for trendiness, must own at least three hundred and seventy-two pairs of khaki pants, and must golf."

"This is my list of qualifications?" He puts his hands on his hips, but his eyes are laughing. Finally.

"Well, not really. You fail at golf." I step into his space, our faces inches apart. "So really, you're hardly qualified at all." I whisper the end, and his hand reaches out, grazes my waist.

"If you're ready, you can follow me." An efficient hostess interrupts, her voice high and official. She click-clacks away. Greg shrugs and motions for me to follow. He doesn't take my hand, and I curse her intrusion.

I double-step to keep up with them in my walking cast. She leads us up to a room and swings open the door. A king-sized bed dominates the room, but the details are intricate: an inset ceiling with detailed crown molding, thick pile carpeting and mahogany furniture, a balcony that overlooks the glittering blue pool, lined with lush palms and hibiscus.

"It's paradise," I breathe, and Greg turns to me appreciatively.

The hostess turns to leave, and I hold up an index finger to Greg. I hobble after her in the hall, shutting the door behind me but throwing the slide lock so it can't latch.

"What if I wanted to pay for golf lessons? Do you do that here?" I whisper to her.

"Yes—" She eyes my arm and leg casts and falters.

"It's not for me. It's for… my boyfriend." I test out the word, here in the privacy of this hallway where the words are mine alone. My cheeks and neck grow hot, and I fight back a smile.

"Then yes. A half-day instruction and fitting is four hundred and fifty dollars, but that includes that day's green fees if you choose to leave the rehearsal areas and pursue the course. Shall I schedule you?"

"Yes." I close my eyes and take a breath. Four hundred and fifty dollars is extravagant. Ridiculous even. My rarely used credit card practically vibrates from inside my purse. I extract it and hand it to her. "But charge it here. It's a gift."

She nods once. "That's fine. Thank you. I'll return your card momentarily." She clacks down the hall, and I slip back into the room. Greg is standing on the balcony, a soft breeze rippling his shirt, his hands gripping the railing. The air smells like water and salt, despite the ocean being miles away, and yet the air is dry. To the right of the glimmering pool, I see the nearly four hundred acres of green.

Quietly, I join him on the balcony, and he turns to me and gives me a half smile.

"Glad you came?" he asks absently.

"Mostly." I'm being honest, and his eyebrows arch up.

"Well, for nearly five hundred a night, I was hoping for more than a mostly." He's joking. I know this, but it gives me a quick fire.

"It could be thousands a night," I shoot back. "But something is up with *you*." I wonder then if I even know him well enough to make that assumption. Maybe he's the quiet type. Maybe travel makes him nervous. "I'm sorry," I amend quickly. "Does traveling stress you?"

His hand covers mine on the railing. "I travel one hundred and fifty days a year. I wouldn't have been in this job for ten years if it did."

"Because you seem…." I search for the right words and fail, so I let the ending hang there, unfinished.

"I'm fine." He pulls me sideways between him and the railing and kisses me hard on the mouth. His hands run up and down my sides, and my uneasiness slides away, forgotten. He smells warm and sunny. I run my hand through his close-shorn hair, tracing the bones of his jaw with my fingertip.

I wrap my air-casted leg around his calf and pull him against me until we're both breathing heavily, and he pulls away, resting his forehead against mine so that our breath mingles. "Except you are going to make it very hard for me to actually go to work."

"Ah, well, that was my hope." I giggle and lean into him. He makes a noise and tucks my hair behind my ear. I nudge him back, just a little, and point toward the green in our peripheral. "Just don't work too hard. You have a golf lesson to take." I study his face. At first his brows knit together in confusion, but then he breaks into a big grin.

"You bought me a golf lesson?" His eyebrows arch, and he leans back, studying me, puzzled.

"I did. Just now, in the hallway with Ms. Clickity Shoes. So make sure to fit it in between all your other activities." I jut my chin in the direction of the bed and twist my mouth.

He laughs. "You're... I can't believe you'd do that."

"It didn't seem like you were going to. And I thought, God, how can you come here and not at least try it?" I shake my head. "It seemed like something you wanted to do but wouldn't have taken upon yourself."

"You're right. I did want to do it. I *do.* And no, I wouldn't have thought to actually do it." He leans out over the railing and studies the landscape. "It's been a long time since I thought about what I want to do. I feel like I spend my whole life thinking about what I have to do. Does that make sense?"

I think of Amy and Lesley. Paula draped over Tig's bar. Pete throwing money on the table because he had to go. Scott and his endless jazz conversations. "More than you could possibly know." I think about the violin and the symphony, which seems a million miles away, almost as if I was a different person.

"Do you have a passion?" I ask suddenly, remembering how I used to spout this, back in high school when well-meaning but obtrusive teachers would cluck at my single focus, my lack of desire for school work or math. They'd talk to Paula in hushed voices as though I couldn't hear them, about devoting more time to my studies—until Paula pulled me out of school altogether and hired a tutor. But I had *passion,* something I was convinced all those gray-pallored, silver-haired schoolmarms wouldn't have known if it tapped them on the shoulder. I was attached to the idea of being a passionate person—until, of course, Nikolai told me I wasn't.

"Passion?" Greg repeats as though he's never heard the word. "Actually, no. Not for anything." He shakes his head, almost dazed. "Is that the saddest thing you've ever heard?"

"No. You're not a hundred, for God's sake. If you want to find a passion, find something. Maybe it's golf?" I cock my head to the side.

"Maybe. You never know unless you try?" He

laughs. "What about you? What will you do while I'm gone?" His face nuzzles against my neck.

I tilt my head toward the water below. "See that? I might not be able to swim in it, but it will sure be nice to lie next to it." I wink and slide out from between the railing and him and, taking his fingertips in my own, lead him to the beckoning white bed.

"You are amazing," he whispers. When he lays me back against the luxury bedding, the blankets nearly swallow us whole, and the breeze dances over my bare skin, raising goose bumps. The sheers lift and fall in the summery air, and Greg leaves a trail of kisses from my neck to my knees. I think about how I was wrong. My life didn't peak at fourteen in the dark and shadowy corners of the Chateau Frontenac.

Despite what I've said to the hostess, I don't know if Greg is my boyfriend. The San Diego trip seemed to be a turning point, one that felt like a definitive line in the sand. Before, we were casually dating, maybe even just exploring. After, he is all I think about, our texting amped up to hourly, phone calls several times a day and lasting late into the night, almost until dawn.

I pressure him to move to Canada. "What do you have keeping you in New Jersey?" I whine, only half joking. I ask a variation of this question regularly. *What do you do there? Why do you live there? Who are your friends?* With variations on the same answers. *My life is so boring—you wouldn't believe.*

I should have been frustrated. I should have been angry. My arm was healing, but slowly. I sit in Nikolai's office, where he strokes the corners of his moustache with thick, patient fingers.

"I think the best course of action is to sit out the remainder of the season." He nods his head as though I've agreed with him. I feel nothing.

"I need money," I blurt and realize only after I say it that it's true. "I'm better now. I'm in physical therapy. I can at least come for rehearsals."

"You can collect disability." He fumbles through some papers on his desk, moves the one-tusked elephant that I swear he put there just for this visit. He's so goddamn pretentious. He pushes the stack of paperwork, curled at the edges and smelling like pipe smoke, across the desk at me with a wide, flat palm.

I tug on a corner, and he doesn't let up. "You don't seem ready to come back." His mouth bows down in a little frown. He's right, maybe. Hard to tell.

I pick at that blasé feeling. Weeks ago, I would have been chomping at the bit to get back. If I'd broken my arm a year ago, I would have been rehearsing the second my arm could withstand the movement, with or without the bow. I would have watched old videos, listened to old recordings of myself. I would have been obsessive about deterioration, loss of dexterity.

I've done none of these things. Instead, I've gone on dates, chatted on the phone, giggled, had sex, played footsies under a restaurant table, texted. I wasn't replacing my lifelong passion with a man. That was a cliché. But I couldn't deny that I now chased Greg with the same fervor I'd used to pursue music. What was the point? It's a lot of work to be given the same feedback over and over.

In the meantime, my ankle brace came off, and every other week, I happily drove the three hours south to Rochester to spend the week with Greg in his company suite. I'd read, watch TV, amble around the box of a hotel room, wait for him to get home. We'd go to dinner, local pubs or dive bars, where we'd spend hours laughing and talking, the hours flying by until the staff would start turning the chairs upside down on the tables.

Thinking about Amy cuts a painful slice beneath my breastbone. I haven't called her, and I hold on to the justification that she hasn't called me. But it isn't holding water anymore.

When I first joined the TSO, Amy was already there. She was loud and bubbly and friends with everyone around her, flirting with the bassoons and pushing her glossy hair off the back of her neck with a long, elegant hand. The conductor at the time was a broad young man named Simon Blunt, graying at the temples but with watchful eyes and a playful streak. Amy teased him mercilessly.

She flung her smile around at everyone but me. When I spoke, she'd narrow her eyes and stare over my shoulder before turning away to talk to someone else. It baffled me, this cold, bizarre shunning. Most of the time, competition in an orchestra hummed underneath but never became outright and nasty. I hadn't known what to make of it. Later, I figured it out. She was the youngest, an enthusiastic darling with a shine. Then I came along, even younger—blonder, a bit ethereal, but with some bite. Intriguing. Politics are everywhere. I endured weeks of this.

My first breakthrough with Amy came at the deli down the street from the orchestra hall. She stood at the register, a sandwich and coffee arranged on a tray in front of her as she scrambled in her purse, panic in her eyes and a blush in her cheeks. I stepped forward and handed the cashier a ten-dollar bill. When she whipped around and saw that it was me, she cocked her head coyly. She muttered thanks and hurried off, snagging a corner table, a two-top with only one chair. I paid for my lunch and followed her.

I grabbed a chair and plunked it down opposite her. She glanced up, surprised.

"So," I said, picking the tomatoes I'd asked them to hold off my roll. "You don't like me much. I don't know why. But it seems like it can't be any real reason. I've never done anything to you. I just got here a few weeks ago." I didn't make eye contact. My bravado was false. Most is.

"I don't dislike you." Her voice was low, but it trickled out unemphatically. It was a lie.

"Hmmm, well." I shrugged and smiled at her. "I bought you lunch so... you have to at least try now."

She said nothing and stared at her plate, all her bubbly confidence deflated. I'd tried to make it better, but I'd inadvertently made it worse. I stood, my half-eaten sandwich limp on the tray. She looked up, and I gave her a weak smile and a little wave.

Out on the sidewalk, I'd breathed in cold air until my lungs hurt.

"Wait!" someone yelled, and I turned.

It was her, her hair flinging left and right as she ran toward me. She stopped, inches away. Too close, invading my personal space. I backed up.

"Let's get a drink, okay? Tonight, after rehearsal. We'll do dinner and drinks. What do you think?" She was breathless and smiling, her cheeks flushed.

I cocked my head to the side. What the hell?

She laughed and waved her hand. "Simon," she said, like that explained everything. "He watches you. I'm being an idiot."

I shrugged. Men paid attention to me on occasion. I was pretty, not beautiful, but tall and blonde and arrestingly direct, so I'd been told. She leaned forward, her hair brushing my cheek, her hand on my shoulder, and whispered into my ear, "I'm sleeping with him."

She backed up and, eyes sparkling, put a finger to her lips. "Shhhh."

Later, at dinner, she'd told me everything: their affair, his flailing marriage, her desire to get married, his desire to escape. We drank and talked late into the night. I'd never had a real girlfriend before, a drinking, giggling, sharing, advice-giving girlfriend. Rehearsals and auditions had been my girlfriends, my boyfriends, my enemies and confidantes. For everything else, there was Paula. Human connection is an instantly addictive drug. It was my heroin.

We lunched at the same deli every week, like spouses paying homage to their relationship. We giggled and cheered when Simon finally left, groaned when Nikolai joined us, gossiped about the third and fourth chairs, rolled our eyes at anyone two minutes late to rehearsal, commiserated over a botched solo. In between, we talked about Paula and Amy's overbearing family, her parents' financial crisis, her sister's competitive streak.

I missed her more than I'd cared to admit.

I'm lying on the bed in Greg's suite, trying to focus on *Big Brother*, but even that doesn't keep my interest. I pick up my cell phone and dial Amy.

She actually answers this time. I drop the phone with a soft *plop* on the bedspread with surprise and scramble to retrieve it.

"Hi! How are you? I was worried about you?" Her sentences tilt up insecurely, and I imagine her perched on the other end, settling down into the big easy chair in her mother's living room. Five years older than me and still living at home. I wonder what it's like to live, fully supported, among people you understand, people you like. I stare at the whitewashed walls of the hotel room and wonder if I'd want that.

"You didn't call." I say this simply, without malice.

"I know. You told me not to, and I was angry at you. I'm not anymore." She rushes on, all her sentences run together, and I hear her breath before her words, one long giant huff of air.

"You were mad at me?" I strike an unintentionally sharp tone.

"Kar, come on, don't. I was. I just thought you were being unfair. No position is guaranteed to anyone, right? Besides, you didn't even seem like you wanted it that badly. I don't know…"

I ponder this. It's not the competition I resented, but the winning. Maybe she's right, and I didn't want it. I don't know. I push the thought away.

"I met someone." It bursts out of me, and I wonder if my whole drive for calling her centered around being able to finally talk to someone about Greg.

"Wait, what about Scott?" She laughs into the phone in a way that means *you tramp* but not seriously. I realize that, yes, I've definitely missed her. A girlfriend, maybe even a best friend. A confidante. Someone to giggle over rum and Cokes with.

"Scott broke up with me. He met someone else, he said. The same night… you won concertmistress. The day before I got into the accident. It was a shitty two days. But… " I let my voice linger. "It's the day I met Greg. So…."

"We need a girls' dinner out, I guess."

"We really do." I pause. "It's only been a month, but I really think I might marry this guy."

"What? That's crazy, Karen!" She pauses and continues seriously. "You don't do this. You don't fall all over a guy, ever. You were lukewarm about Scott on a good day. What gives?"

"I don't know," I say slowly. "You're right, I don't. He's different. This is different. I know, I sound like a teenager. I feel like one."

"Does he feel that way about you?"

"I don't know. I think so?" I scratch my arm. "He can be hard to read. I don't think he's had a ton of affection in his life, so he can be standoffish."

"Sounds like someone else I know," Amy comments wryly.

I smirk into the phone. We agree to meet up when I get back, and I hang up, feeling lighter than I have in weeks. That makes me think, oddly, of Paula, and my finger hovers over her name in my contacts list. Before I can pull the trigger, my phone vibrates in my hand. Greg.

Meet me downstairs! I'm starving! xo.

And just like that, Paula is forgotten.

It's been eight weeks. The cast is off. My arm, my skinny, hairy, wizened arm, is free. I flex my fingers, pulling my thumb to my forefinger and bowing across an imaginary set of strings.

"See? Good as new! Nothing gained, nothing lost." The orthopedist is clipped and efficient, anxious to scoot me on my way.

"Nope. Just my career," I say cavalierly. He looks startled, and I laugh self-consciously. "I didn't want that anyway. No worries." I hop down from the table, already thinking about what witty quip I'll text to Greg, maybe a picture, maybe a sexy message. My ankle is new again. My arm is healed. All my broken parts are put back together.

Outside, I settle for a quick picture of my un-casted arm and a flirty text, a combination of informational and sexy. *Next week should be fun ;).*

Before he can reply, my phone buzzes in my hand. It's a number I don't recognize, and I stare at it in confusion.

I click "accept."

"Is this Karen Caughee?" a brisk voice asks on the other line. In the background, I hear a loud clattering, almost like the din in a restaurant. The voice is androgynous, a reedy, haughty tone, and I can't make out what they're saying.

I stop in the street and cover my ear with my hand. "I'm sorry, I can barely hear you."

The voice comes into sharp focus, definitely female. "I *said* is your mother Paula Caughee?"

I close my eyes. "Yes. Who is this?"

"This is Officer Minks. We're holding your mother in lockup down here at the police station."

"Oh, God. What did she do?" My gut sinks like a stone. She once got into a bar fight. Imagine a fifty-year-old woman clawing at the face of a younger, fitter, thirty-something while her friends tittered around her. My mother was a joke at Tig's. I wondered this time if she'd actually hurt someone, caught that young McGill U grad right in the cornflower blue of her iris. I cringed.

"Driving under the influence, ma'am." Not a fight, then. I let out a breath slowly. The voice continued, both warning and droning, somehow. "You'd better come quickly."

"What's her bail?" I press my hand to my forehead.

"Four thousand dollars."

I don't *come quickly* as instructed by the desk sergeant. I go back to my apartment. I spend about a half hour on Google and look up sentences and bail rates for DUIs. I look up treatment facilities. I arm myself with information.

I also need to calm down. My blood roils hot and fast under my skin, and if I focus even on the idea of Paula, my vision swims with rage. How dare she?

I consider, briefly, leaving her. Calling Pete: *your turn.* Could I do that? He'd get her. They'd sit in the cold, stainless steel cube of a cell, and Pete would commiserate. He wasn't pushed to any breaking point with Paula. He still calls her Mom. He thinks she's damaged but not ruined and certainly not capable of breaking anyone else. He considers her like a broken-winged bird, wild eyed and scared. To me, she's a mountain lion: animalistic and angry. Beautiful to look at, impossible to love.

Her withdrawal as my mother happened slowly and seemingly overnight. One day, I looked up, and she hadn't come to a show in days. The days turned into weeks, and she stopped asking. Dad had left, Pete had gone away to college, and her abandonment felt swift and pure, as if maybe she'd never really been there in the first place. Her abandonment was made all the more sharp against the backdrop of Amy with her family in tow, literally four times as supportive as my own. Six, sometimes eight of them: parents and siblings, and aunts and uncles and cousins. She had a veritable tribe.

At one time, Paula sat across from me at Chateau Frontenac, tipping her hand in a *sit up straight* motion and silently reminding me to remove my elbows from the table. She visibly held her breath during auditions, standing in the front row, taut as a violin string. That mother—the one I knew—was gone. I'd spent the end of my teen years and my early twenties wondering: If I'd been better, faster, if I'd been accepted to the Toronto Philharmonic as an over-eager nineteen-year-old instead of turned down, would she have drunk less? If she'd drunk less, would she have been less volatile? Her violence was fueled by liquor and suspicion of my father's infidelities. Any object within arm's reach—a broomstick, a glass, a kitchen chair—became the outlet.

I moved out one Sunday with only the most cursory of notice. The Thursday before, I'd made dinner, some chicken and Campbell's soup casserole, waxen and gluey, and called Mom for dinner. She appeared, bleary-eyed but pleasant. I was relieved, because pleasant wasn't always on the dinner menu. Sometimes, she was caustic, sarcastic, or even downright incensed. We ate in silence. She never asked about anything: my career, dates, friendships. It was as if, when Dad moved out, he'd left behind only an apathy that no amount of second-tier talent or Ritz cracker casseroles could ameliorate.

"I'm moving on Sunday." I stopped, inhaled, put down my fork, and blotted my mouth with a one-ply paper towel. "I'm moving out," I repeated slowly, so she'd understand. She blinked twice, her mouth opening and closing like a fish on a hook.

"Why?" She lifted her chin at me, a gesture of defiance, but her eyes were wild.

"Because." My fork clanked against my plate, louder than I'd intended. "This"—I waved my hand back and forth between us—"is not a life. We barely even speak to each other. I can't live this way."

"You sound just like your father." She gave a high-pitched, chittering laugh, almost hyena-like. "Are you cheating on me, too? Do you have another mother?"

"God, no. One is enough." I mumbled this, my mouth glommed full of pasty food, but she caught it, and her eyes narrowed.

"I didn't know I've been such a hardship to you, Karen." Her jaw went very still, in that way my father used to call "the green sky before the tornado." It was a warning, a calm before the storm, that tight clicking of her lower jaw, tooth against tooth, breathing only through her nose.

I said nothing, just sat and drank water as she tinkled the ice cubes around her vodka tumbler. I watched her glass, and she watched my face watching her glass. She stood, took her plate and drink to the sink, and dumped the ice cubes down the drain. She turned, stared at me for a moment, and shook her head as though she didn't recognize me.

On her way out, she dumped her dinner in the trashcan, glass plate and all. She stood in the doorway, palms braced against the trim, and did her dragon nose breathing routine.

"You know," she said. *Puff. Puff.* "It was me—not your father—who gave you your career. You're just like him, you know. Neither of you appreciate what I've done for either one of you. You can have each other."

I'm ashamed to admit I felt almost proud of the comparison at the time. My father left, sure, but as a victim. She practically chased him out. It's easy to remain a hero from a safe distance traversed only by occasional birthday cards and echoing, silence-filled phone calls. He was a pointillist painting, a Seurat, perfectly formed from a safe distance. It would be at least five years before I'd realize my father didn't just leave her. He'd left us. In that five years, he'd accumulated almost hero status, the one who got out. I wanted to be like him.

Later, I fished the glass plate out of the trash,

washed the dishes, and dried them. The kitchen looked the way it had for the last fifteen years, as long as I had memories: dark wooden cabinets, Formica countertops, patterned linoleum. Dated but clean. Gleaming surfaces, like Mom always liked them. Before it smelled like liquor, my entire childhood smelled like lemon Pledge.

I moved out three days later with little fanfare: a friend's pick-up truck, some bungee cords, and the contents of my bedroom. Mom never came out of her room, not even to say good-bye. I stood at her bedroom door, my fingertips resting on the door handle. I jiggled it one way then the other. It was locked.

Four thousand dollars. I pick up my phone, rolling it around in my palms. My fingers decide for me by dialing the number. Shockingly, he picks up. "Pete?" I say. "Mom's in jail. You'd better go get her because I'm not."

CHAPTER 8

"**I**'M READY TO COME BACK." I sit firmly across from Nikolai, who strokes his mustache, curling it around his pinkie, and pats his wobbling jowl.

"We've been over this, yes?" He leans forward across the desk and taps the flat calendar. "The season is more than half over. Sit out then re-audition for your chair. That's what we decided."

"That's what *you* decided." I slap my palm across the big March page, and he jumps back, just a little.

"Karen," he says in a way that he means to be soothing but is anything but. "You'll be back in the fall. Come to rehearsals three days a week for now. In the meantime, take a vacation. You're healed, no?"

I ponder the word. *Heal: to make whole, or healthy.* I remain silent.

"No matter," he continues as if I've responded. "Take a trip. Come back when you're ready. Practice. We are traveling to New York City next week. Come, be an alternate. Then join us again at the end of August."

August. When the new recruits would start. Weeks before the returning members. My career is going backward.

I sit back in my chair and stare at him defiantly. "Do I have a choice?"

"It does not seem so, no," he says softly.

I stand to leave, but he keeps talking. "I believe in balance, Karen. In joy. Find joy, and come back. You'll be a better musician for it."

I leave abruptly with a curt good-bye. I swing open his office door and almost walk right into a man I don't recognize hovering outside.

"Were you listening in?" I snap.

He steps back, startled. "No, I, uh, had a meeting with Mr. Maslak."

"He's all yours." I wave toward Nikolai's office with one hand.

"I'm Calloway. Cal for short." He holds out his hand and smiles, sideways and shy, and oh, God, he's flirting with me. I back up, but he keeps talking. "I was recently hired as a replacement trombone. Are you new?"

"Apparently." I turn away and feel bad for being so flippant. I turn back, half-facing him. He's tall, lanky, and sandy haired with a smattering of freckles across his face and arms. "I'm sorry, it's been… a day. I'll see you around, okay?"

He nods and waves as if I'm the friendliest person around, and who knows, maybe I am. Orchestras can be particularly exclusive. I wave back half-heartedly. I have a summer to plan.

June ascends like a big ball of fire—thick, wet, record-breaking fire. For the first time in my life, I'm free. Free of the arduous rehearsal schedules, free of teaching classes, free of the stress of not doing enough. I want the spring break I never had, the summer fling I never got, holed up in hot, underfunded university rehearsal halls.

I drag Greg to Prince Edward Island, and the temperatures soar into the nineties, almost unheard of in that area. We take a bicycle tour of the area lighthouses and visit an Angora bunny farm. We eat same-day-fresh lobster every night and get drunk on local wine.

We bring a blanket to the beach, watch the sunset, and lie in the sand talking until midnight. The waves lick the edges of the blanket. I've never seen so many stars.

"You find out you're going to die in a year. What do you do?" I trace circles on his palm with my fingertip, continuing our ongoing game. Random questions, truthful answers. Anything, any time. I want to know every small piece of him with voracity.

"This."

It's dark, and I can't see his face. "That's not entirely truthful." I am whispering, soft and reverent, under the black velvet sky. "What else?"

"The last time you cried." He leapfrogs over me, dodging his answer.

"Oh, that's easy. When Pete bailed Paula out and called me to tell me she was okay, but she wrecked her car. I hung up and cried."

"Did I know that?"

"I'm sure I texted you."

He gently pinches my thumb, teasingly, and nudges me with his elbow.

"Do you want kids?" I ask.

Silence for a beat. "I can't imagine not. Do you?"

"I don't know. I worry about taking care of other people. What if I'm like Paula? What if I don't know how to mother?" This is what panics me when I try to picture a future, a marriage, children.

"It's an instinct, not a skill."

"Exactly. What if I don't have it?"

He takes my chin in his fingers and kisses me lightly. "Impossible. I'm not worried about that, and look at my mother. Besides, you're too gentle and kind. "

I snort. I've never been called *gentle* in my life. My turn. "What else do you like about me?"

"Everything." His answer is quick and sure. I playfully punch him with the side of my fist.

"Too glib. Answer for real."

"Okay. I like that you're passionate about your music. I like that you're spontaneous, and you make me laugh. You never get too bogged down with worry or regret. I like that you hold yourself to a higher moral standard. I like that you're mad at Paula for the decisions she's made. You live in that condo like it's temporary because you don't really like it, yet you never complain about it." He pulls me up until I'm straddling him. He runs his hands up and down my arms. "I like how you hold people accountable and even that you don't let people in, although I think you should. I like that you're learning how. You're independent and think you don't need anyone, but I think you actually do. You're tougher than you want to be and stronger than you think you are."

I push his shirt up, kiss his chest, and nuzzle against his warm skin. My lips graze his neck, his ear. His words feel like pins, poking sharp against the vulnerable skin of an overripe peach. I want him to stop talking, and at the same time, I want him to talk forever. I want to hear all the things he knows about me that I don't know myself, and only then will I feel real. And whole. And healed.

"I love you," I whisper. My hands fumble against his belt. The beach is deserted. I slip out of my sundress. I want the warmth of his skin against my skin. I want it all. Forever.

Something has changed. It's barely perceptible. The summer is fading into fall, bringing with it the promise of a new symphonic season. August looms on the horizon, and with each passing day, Nikolai's voice becomes louder and clearer in my head. I've been horrendously lax in my practicing, and I feel the stiffness of my fingers as they find their way to the positions a fraction of a beat too late.

I text Greg and hear nothing back for hours. This started a few weeks ago, and I don't know how to fix it, how to find our way back to that night at Prince Edward Island when he could see every piece of me, every cell, every artery, every synapse of my brain. I want it back, and the idea that I'm looking into the back end of it sends me panicking. I'm texting too much, too often. I've even started calling. He picks up, distracted and faintly annoyed, I can tell, even when he's trying not to be. "*I'll call you, okay?*" He says his job is so demanding. The more I reach out, the more he pulls back, and if I think about it, I can't breathe.

"When are you coming back to Toronto?" I haven't seen him in four weeks, the longest we've gone. "I miss you."

"I know, me too. Me too." He says it with conviction, but he doesn't say it because he never says, "I love you, too." Except for one time, when he climaxed and breathed it right into my mouth, and it was the sweetest thing I ever tasted. If I voiced all this, it would make me sound crazy and would lead him to sigh, these big empty Greg sighs. I want to be the Karen he thinks I am, the one who is independent and needs no one. But this is the problem: I let him in. And now he's going away, fading slowly into the night, like my father. The way even Paula did, if not physically, then mentally.

I ask him if he's all right, and he sighs. "I'm fine, Karen. Not every day can be your best day lived, right? Some days just... pass. Or does that not happen to you?"

"You have this crazy misconception that I'm over here living some kind of fantasy every day. I do nothing. I watch television. I read. I try to practice the violin, but I'm mostly frustrated at how I've slid, so I ignore it and pretend it doesn't exist."

"I'm sorry. I get jealous. You have a career. I have a job." He whispers this into the phone at two a.m. "You don't know that you're lucky."

"You don't understand that I work, too. That just because it's music and not corporate, it's not all artistic and fun and easy. Nothing about it is easy." I slap my palm against my bed, tired. "If you want to do something else, do something else. It's not rocket science. But nothing just happens on its own, you know."

He pauses. "You say this like it's simple. My life is entrenched here."

"So untrench it. But don't spend half your life unhappy. Happiness is a thing that is nurtured."

"What if I moved away? Would you come with me?"

"Moved where?" I ask suspiciously. His voice is tinny, like he's talking into a paper towel roll.

"They might transfer me to China."

My heart thuds in my throat. "I can't go to China." My life is here, my job, the job that I've worked my whole life for, and no matter how up in the air it feels right now, I can't just leave. My mother, God, who would take care of Paula? Not Pete.

"I know. Me either. It was just an idea."

"Are you okay?" I ask. He sounds unmoored, floating.

"Maybe. Forget China, okay? It was a dumb idea."

"Just come back soon." If I see him again, I'm sure I can fix whatever is wrong, whatever has come unglued when I wasn't paying attention.

He does come back, almost six weeks after Prince Edward, and I'm looking at my last week of freedom, the summer already taking on the orangey-hazy glow of hindsight. I'm back to rehearsing three to four hours a day in preparation for next week, but I want this last week of summer love.

"Maybe I'll just come stay with you," Greg says. He never does that. He's always gotten a hotel. He's never not had a home base away from my apartment that he can leave to, and I've never asked him not to. I hold my breath and want to ask why. Is it because he's trying to save us? Move us forward? Move away, halfway across the world, and leave me here?

It's stuck there like an itch now. I want to ask him all the girl-questions: What are we? Where are we going? Do we have a future? But I'm scared of his answers. Then he says it so easily—"I'll just stay with you"—that I think maybe I've dreamed up the last few weeks, made mountains out of molehills.

I plan an elaborate dinner: shrimp carbonara and crusty bread, dry, expensive wine, and perfectly crisped radicchio. I buy a pricey, black slinky dress that shows more than a hint of cleavage and a push-up bra to go with it. I pull out all the stops, demanding his love with food and sex until it's practically a bribe.

I buy a small sleeve of golf balls and wrap it with ribbon. On the back, I scrawl: *Passions must be nurtured.* I want to show him that it's just one step— one hop-skip—to picking up a hobby he didn't have before. That your life can change incrementally. It doesn't have to change all at once.

When I let him in, the candles are lit. His eyes grow wide.

"Hi," I say shyly.

"Hi." His eyes travel down to my toes and back up. I've shocked him. "You look…" He crosses the threshold and kisses me. I wrap my arms around his neck, press my body against his, and feel his response. He drops his small overnight bag on the floor and kicks the door shut with his heel. His hands are hot through the silk, and I run my fingertips through his hair. He lifts me up and carries me to the kitchen table, where I giggle and blow out the candles before he sets me down. I unbuckle his belt and pull him into me before either of us can even get undressed. I pull him against me so fast our teeth clank, and he laughs into my mouth. When we come, I whisper *I love you* into his ear, unplanned and unbidden.

He pants, his lips hot and wet on my collarbone,

and kisses up my neck. "God, you're amazing. This is not how I thought the night would start out." He laughs against my skin, and I run my fingertip up the back of his neck. He shivers against me. I love that I can do that. I gently push him back, and he looks around, laughing.

"Are you cooking?" His eyebrows arch.

"I can cook." I straighten my dress and shoot him an indignant look. "We just always eat out."

"I never said you couldn't cook, and you've spent a large part of our relationship in traction."

It would be a good segue. *Our relationship?* But I let the moment hang until it fades away, unable to decide how to press it.

I turn the stove back on and simmer the sauce. He comes up behind me. His hands rest on my hips, his dress shoes flanking my bare feet. I love this, our domesticity, more than anything else about us. I love playing house, imagining for a moment that he doesn't live hundreds of miles away, in another country, entrenched in a life or whatever he said the other night. It's a fun fantasy.

He nuzzles the back of my head. "Do you mind if I take a shower?"

I shake my head and wave my hand. "Of course not, *mi casa, su casa* and all that."

I hear him pad to the bathroom, and the water rushes on, up the wall behind me. I lean forward, steadying myself against the sink, and take a deep breath. My eye catches on his overnight bag in front of the door, and I have an idea.

Greg's always been proud of his ability to pack light. His bag is small, only slightly bigger than a bowling bag. I grab the sleeve of golf balls off the table and unzip it, feeling a little guilty. I want him to find them tomorrow morning, while he's dressing and I'm sleeping, when he's at his most bored—or frustrated with his job, or feeling stuck. I want him to remember that I think it's possible.

I unzip the side pocket and fumble around, looking for his toothbrush. My fingertips slide on something smooth and metallic, and I pull it out. Examine it. Turn it around in my fingers, my heart picking up speed with every passing second, a dull thud behind my eyes. It's heavier than I would think, silver-gray, battered and weathered. I can still feel his weight on me, his shudder between my thighs, his mouth on my neck, his breath in my ear. *I love you.*

It's a man's wedding ring.

CHAPTER 9

HE'S WHISTLING WHEN HE COMES out of the shower, one of my faded beach towels slung lazily off his hips. He's fucking whistling.

"I'll need my bag," he jokes and kisses me on the crown of my head, oblivious. He stops, cocks his head, stares at me like he's seeing me for the first time. "Are you okay? What's wrong?"

I hold up the ring between my thumb and my forefinger. The color drains from his face, he swallows, and in that moment, I know it's true. My brain was frantic, filling in the gaps with some tragic story: an accident from his past, an ex-wife, a deceased wife, anything. It's truly amazing the story your mind can spin in one panicked second. But none of that was true. What's real and true is that Greg is *married,* not past tense, not divorced, not widowed. I can see our whole relationship in his white face. I see his furtive two a.m. phone calls, his cryptic texts, his seemingly random reticence interlaced with moments where he was just *so happy* to see me. His business trips, the way he never stayed here, the way he didn't talk about his life much, the way he called it boring.

We stand off, him trying to look somewhat dignified in my towel and me trying not to vomit. I smell the shrimp burning on the stove. I hold the ring out to him, and he takes it, tucks it into his fist. I walk to the kitchen, turn off the burner, and walk back to the living room, where he still stands woodenly next to his overnight bag.

"It's true, right? You're married." I stand in front of him with my arms crossed over my chest. I'm suddenly overly aware of what I'm wearing, and I'm freezing. "You're married."

"Yes." He doesn't offer an explanation or an excuse, because I would hate him for that. I hate him enough as it is, but some pathetic mumbling about a bad marriage or money troubles or horrible sex lives or whatever else married couples fight about would push me right over the edge.

"But." I swallow. "You don't wear a ring. You weren't wearing one the first night we met. I would have noticed."

"I...." His voice fades, and his eyes dart wildly around the room. He sighs. "The first time I met you—I had taken it off that week. To see what it felt like. I... was thinking of leaving. I haven't been happy for a long time. And after that, I didn't know how to put it back on." He splays his hands out helplessly. "How to tell you."

"How long have you been married?" I hiss this.

"Ten years." His voice is hoarse, and my mind

flits impossibly on the idea that it might be okay. He could leave his wife. No. *No.*

"This is a thing you do, then? Just skip from affair to affair?" I'm wondering who else he's slept with. I don't even think about his wife. *His wife.* The anger is white hot behind my eyes, and my chest aches. Oh, my God. I've never been so stupid. Anyone would have seen this. All his stupid vague answers that I just let go—on some level, I must have known. "I'm so stupid."

He takes a step forward and reaches out to touch my arm. "No. Karen, no. You're the first—"

I swat his hand away. "Don't you touch me. You don't get to touch me." My temper flares, the one that made me throw the mug at Scott, and I close my eyes to steady my breathing. My pulse throbs in my temples. "Why?"

"Why what?" Greg asks, dumbly.

"Why did you pick me to screw over? Why did you make me fall in love with you? Why did you let me do this?" I realize that I'm yelling at him, and I don't care. I pursued him, and he let me. He takes a step back, his eyes wide. "Why wouldn't you tell me? You tried to tell me. That first night, you said, 'Wait, I have to tell you something.' Was this the something? Is this my fault?"

He shakes his head. "It's not what I wanted, either. Don't you see that? This has been killing me." He tries to touch my arm again, and I slap his hands away, paddling at him with both hands. I can't even stand to think about his hands on my skin. "I didn't set out to do this. I fell in love with you, too, and I didn't know that it was possible to love two people at the same time. But you and Claire are so different—"

"Claire?"

"My wife."

I sit on the floor, the strap of my dress hanging off the side of my shoulder, and I don't even bother to fix it. "I don't want to know her name!" I pound the floor with my fist. I don't want to know anything about her or his life. I don't want his excuses or his lies about his unhappy—or maybe happy—marriage. Her name, Claire, sits under my tongue like sand in an oyster shell that will never pearl, gritty and bitter, and I swallow it. *His fucking wife.*

"Karen, I'm sorry. Please." He's crying, too, and he sits next to me, not touching me because he knows better now.

"I don't care about your sorry. Why?" I stand up and pace around the room, to the couch, the TV. I pick up a candle, put it back. Hard. The television rattles. "Why did you seek me out?"

"I didn't seek you out! Not really. I was attracted to you at the bar, and then you got hit, and everything snowballed. I wanted to help you, and no one else was helping you—"

"So I was a fucking charity case to you? Did you sleep with me out of pity?"

"Karen, stop. That's ridiculous. I didn't set out for this to happen. It just happened."

123

"No. It didn't just happen. You knew you were married, and I did not. You let this happen."

He's silent for a moment. "You're right. I let this happen." His voice is soft and hoarse, and I'm so angry I can feel it vibrating all the way down to my toes, but still, somehow, I want to touch him. I want to reach out and comfort him. It makes no sense, and I won't do it. I refuse. His back is bare, and I stare at it and remember kissing up the dip in his spine, my hands splayed across his shoulder blades, my nakedness against his nakedness, all my *I love yous* whispered into nothingness, into the wind because I was saying them to someone who should not, could not love me back.

"I loved you." I push the heel of my hand into my forehead. "I still do love you. And that's the shit of it all. I still do, and I'm going to for a long time. You have to live with this. You hurt me. You did this." I take a deep breath, ragged and shaking. "I let you know me. Now you know me when no one else does, and you have to deal with that."

"Karen, please. I'm so sorry. I love you, too. I couldn't tell you. I couldn't say that. Can you understand?"

"But you can tell me now?" I stand across the room, my arms folded tightly across my middle.

He opens his mouth, closes it. "I don't know. I've been falling apart inside for months. I couldn't tell you, but then sometimes it seemed like you were my…. salvation. I couldn't leave this. My marriage is… was…"

I hold up my hand. "I don't want to know about your marriage." But as soon as I say it, I realize it's a total lie. I want to know everything about his marriage. I want him to justify staying here with me, for this to continue. I want him to leave her. I am the other woman. This happens in movies, dammit, and he needs to leave her.

"Would you leave her? Your wife?"

His leg peeks out from under the towel, his thigh, all the way up to his hip, and it's so vulnerable and pale, the part that no one sees. The intimacy of it is shocking, all that coarse, light hair curling around the skin of his thigh. He stands and picks up the bag. His movements are slow, underwater and thick. He walks to the bathroom, and the door clicks shut. I hear him getting dressed, a soft, muffled rustling. I imagine him coming out of the bathroom, holding me, kissing me, wanting only me. I dig my nails into my arm. It's so goddamn pathetic that I would want that. Where is my self-respect? I channel Amy. She'd shake my shoulders and say, "What is wrong with you?" She'd never grovel for a man, married or not. At least, she never did.

Everything. Everything is wrong with me. I want this, more than anything. I want him to choose me, to pick me, to grab me and kiss me and make love to me on the floor of my living room with no secrets and no lies. I want him to tell me it's always been me, all along, and he didn't know true love until he met me. I want him to tell me he's leaving her. He'll move to Toronto. He'll marry me.

The door to the bathroom opens, and his bag is zipped. It's closed. Over. Passion doesn't stop to zip a bag.

"Would you leave her?" I ask again. This time, I square my shoulders because I know the answer.

"Karen, please don't do this. I love you. I love both of you. I didn't know that was possible—"

"Stop saying that. Just stop it. It's easy. Yes or no? Will you leave your wife? For me?" I don't even think of her, of who she is or what she wants, or if she knows that her husband has been having an affair. I don't consider her at all, actually, and I can't because if I think of who she might be, if she has dark hair or long hair, or short hair, or if she is thin or curvy or voluptuous like Scott's Rosa, or bony-thin like me, I might come undone. Right there, I think I could come undone.

She is a flat, paper cardboard person to me, the outline of a woman with no personality. I can't think of her, whether she likes to read or play chess or plays piano or writes poetry. I can't ask if she is mousy or shy or loud or abrasive or flirty or prim. I don't want to know any of these things. I just need to know one thing. *Will he leave her for me?*

"No." He reaches out to touch me again, and this time I let him, his hand falling heavy and awkward on my shoulder. When I look at his face, he's crying real, fat tears. I've never seen a man cry before, not Pete or Scott or my father. I touch his face. My hand comes away wet.

I sob, curled into a ball, my face shoved between

my knees. My dress bunches up around my waist and the carpet is rough and scratchy on my bare bottom. I don't even care what Greg can see, how I must look to him. I wonder if his wife is undignified or emotional. No. I don't want to know anything about her. She is a cardboard person. "You need to leave."

"Please, Karen. Not like this, I can't leave you like this." He's choking and inching toward me, trying to touch me. I kick at him.

"Just get out. Now." And then I lean toward him and scream it in his face. "Now!" He backs away slowly, and I can tell I've made this easier by losing my cool, by coming undone. No guy likes the crazy chick, the one who screams and kicks and hits and bites. I'm not usually her, but I think of my temper and my broken thrown mugs.

He picks up his bag and leaves in two easy steps. The door closes softly behind him. I lean against it, wondering if he's on the other side, waiting for me to open it. But I won't—I can't—look through the peephole. I don't hear him walk away. I go to the bathroom, take his towel that he's hung neatly over the towel rod, and bring it to my nose. It's still damp and smells like his soap. I hold it against my face to muffle the sound of my sob. If he's in the hallway, he won't hear me. I bite into it, the terry cloth between my teeth, the bitter residue of men's shower soap popping on my tongue.

I stare at the door and fight against all the

muscles in my body not to run across the room, fling it open, and call him back. Instead, I sit on the floor and stare at the door, wrapped in a wet towel, and I cry.

I wonder if I'll ever see him again.

CHAPTER 10

THE BUS RIDE TO NEW York is six hours long, and I sleep for much of it, alternately gazing out the window and trying to hide the fact that I'm crying. My stomach slides around inside, sick and cramping. Amy sits next to me but doesn't say much. I tell her the bare bones of what has happened with Greg, and she responds with a soft cluck of her tongue and an "*I'm so sorry.*" The trip will be a reprieve, I tell myself. Greg has been gone a week, and I've become hopelessly addicted to crime drama shows. I watch one after the other: *CSI, Law and Order, NCIS, Criminal Minds.* My head is so full of murder and violence, I jump at every little noise in the house, every bang from the apartments downstairs or next door.

We have four performances and a matinee, a visiting orchestra playing for a Vivaldi festival at Lincoln Center. I miss performing. I miss standing on the stage at the end of a show, the applause thundering in my ears and under my feet. I sit out the performances but watch from the wings, and my chest aches. I miss Greg.

"I'm glad you're back." When I turn around, Calloway stands in the wings, post-show, his trombone resting against his leg. He gives me a sideways smile, and I smile back weakly.

"I'm glad I'm back, too. It's weird, but it's good." I'm putting away my unused violin and bow, tucking it into the velvet-lined case and Velcroing shut all the elastic to keep it from moving around in the undercarriage of the bus. I turn the screw on the bow twice to loosen the hair. It's been mostly unused, but it feels good to go through the motions, packing and unpacking, polishing the wood with Shar, the sharp citrus odor stinging my nostrils. I inspect the strings, replacing one, and refill the Dampit with water. I've always been meticulous when it comes to maintenance, and returning to it feels ritualistic and comfortable, my hands and my mind focused and busy.

Cal hovers, searches for what to say next, and I don't help him. "Long break?"

"Maybe? Feels both too long and too short." I shrug. "I haven't gone this long without performing since I was ten."

He laughs. "Me too. It's in our blood." He taps his fingertips against the curve of his horn. "Did you miss it?"

"I don't know. Yes and no. I guess I'm a little lost as to what I want." I didn't mean to offer that, but I realize then that it's true. I do miss performing.

"Have you considered teaching?"

"No. Teaching is what people do when they can't hack it here."

"That's not true," he protests, but it dies in his throat because he knows it's a lie. He shifts his weight one way then the other. I inspect the fingerboard until he sighs and says, "Talk to ya later," and wanders away.

"Who's that again?" Amy whispers and nods in Calloway's direction.

"Calloway. He's new." I snap the clasps on the case and turn to face her, but she's craning her neck, peering around me where Cal wandered.

"He's cute."

"He seems nice. Go for it." I take a deep breath and turn toward the exit. The buses wait, ready to take us home. *Home.*

"I might," she murmurs. When I turn back, she's gone, and I spy her chatting with Cal, her hand resting on his arm. He laughs at something she says.

I board the bus and sit alone, which actually feels like a relief.

The deadbolt has been replaced. It's the first thing I notice as I stand on Paula's front step, inspecting the chipped and peeling black paint of her front door. The overnight bag in my hand feels heavy and stupid, and I don't know what I'm doing here. I almost walk away. I imagine going back to my empty apartment, watching another hour of *NCIS*.

I'm here because I can't be home. I'm here because I need my mother, and she needs me, whether she knows it or not.

I've been back from New York for three weeks. Greg has been gone a little over a month. The hollow, empty rattling in my gut is lessening but not going away. I never believed in the physical pain of a broken heart, but I realize now it was because I'd never had one. I know Greg isn't coming back, and I'm certainly not chasing after him. I sent one wayward text a week ago, and it came back to me. I called his number a few times, but all I got back was a tinny voice suggesting I check the number and try again. He isn't leaving his wife for me, and the night he left my apartment is likely the last time I'll ever see him. Sometimes, I wonder if I made him up.

I've thrown myself into rehearsals, trying to recapture the skill I know I've lost. My life, by all outward appearances, is back on track. It's my insides that are a mess. Cal's words, "*why don't you teach?*" rattle around my brain, banging against the inside of my skull, demanding my attention. I am plagued with memories of Greg: everything from the way he murmured lightly in his sleep, his fingertips grazing across his lips, to the way he always let me spear the last shrimp from his plate. I have one photo strip, from the shopping mall downtown, that shows our faces pressed together, laughing, kissing. I miss, most of all, someone to be silly with. I think of Scott with his high energy and racing thoughts and how we never did that. We were always so focused.

And now, I wish Greg had been a bit more sensible. We've been so stupid.

I have decisions to make, and I need my mother.

I ring the bell, twice. I flash on a vision of Paula passed out on her bed in the clothes she wore the night before, one arm dangling off the bed, her earrings tangled in her hair. It's noon, but it's happened before.

"Hold on!" Paula yells from inside, and I hear the new dead bolt slide out of place. She opens the door, and her mouth sags. She couldn't look more shocked if I was a clown with a party bag.

"Hi." I try to smile, but it dies somewhere mid-cheek.

She puts a hand to her mouth. "Did you come to yell at me?" She closes her eyes. "Because… I can't do this. Fight with you, I mean."

"Nope." I hold up my overnight bag. "I'm here to stay. For a few days."

"I don't need a babysitter, Karen. I'm sober."

I almost snort but catch myself. I study her. Her skin is clear. The fog that had settled over her irises the past few years—a gray-green cloud over the blue—is gone. Her cheeks are pink. She's wearing ChapStick, not bright-red lipstick, feathered and smeared from the night before. Her eyelashes are bare. She's wearing a chic tracksuit and a pair of bright white sneakers. New.

I haven't seen her for two months, and by God, she *is* sober. Her chin juts defiantly as she dares me to argue with her.

"Why are you here?" Her shoulders round, and her eyes narrow defensively.

"Because I need you." I take a deep breath.

"Bullshit. You haven't needed me a day in your life." She laughs, dry and barky.

"Well," I try to come up with the right words: the true, honest words. That's always been our problem, Paula's and mine. So little of what we've said to each other has been genuine. I haven't had empathy for Paula for as long as I can remember. "You're my mother. I'm your daughter." I square my shoulders and hold her gaze.

She is smaller than me, slighter than me, and has always seemed younger. She steps forward and folds me into her arms. Her scrawny, veined arms, usually adorned with gold bracelets and clattering costume jewelry, today are startlingly bare. I rest my cheek on her pointy shoulder. We stand like that for a moment, and I revel in the feeling of hugging my mother, something I haven't done in a very long time. I feel her ribs against my fingertips, through the cotton of her shirt. She smells like baby powder and laundry detergent and not a bit like vodka. Nothing about it feels familiar.

"You left me in jail," she finally says.

"I know." I sniff against her shoulder. I don't apologize because I'm not sorry, and I'm trying on this real-and-true thing.

"I'm going to be a better mother, Karen." She pats my shoulder, too casual about this admission.

She's never acknowledged that she was anything bu a perfect mother. I don't breathe, and I don't know what to say back.

She steps back and holds the door open. I peer inside. The house looks clean, like the house from my childhood. From the far reaches of the kitchen, I smell a pot roast, and I almost expect to see Daddy at the counter, reading the paper.

"Can I stay for a few days?" I hold up my overnight bag.

"Not like I'd throw you out into the street." She smirks, and I know this is Paula being Paula, trying every which way to let me know that I've hurt her, neglected her, that all the fissures in our relationship are my fault. In the past, I would have snapped back at her, muttered some insult under my breath. I bite my tongue and walk past her, into the house.

"Did Pete fix the door?"

"He's been around once a week to do some light repairs for me. This house is too much by myself." She pats her hair into place and looks around.

"How long have you been sober?" I ask her, partially out of meanness because old habits die hard and also because, to Paula, sober was a temporary lifestyle, the way normal people refer to holidays. *Oh, it's Christmas. I haven't quite gotten to the PTA newsletter this month.*

"Since the day you left me in jail." She walks into the kitchen, and I follow, dropping my bag next to the couch where Daddy used to stow his briefcase.

I wonder how many times she's going to work it in because I've been here five minutes, and the ticker is up to two.

"You've said this before." I say it gently, not trying to be mean.

"I know. But…" She pours me iced tea and avoids my eyes, but I can see a small smile playing at her lips. "I've gone to AA."

I almost drop my glass. Paula always called AA *Arrogant Assholes* and claimed that if you ever found her in the dark basement of a rec center, you could just kill her because she'd already lost her soul.

She smirks a little, like she enjoys the look on my face. "So tell me. Why are you really here?"

I take a long drink of my iced tea. It tastes freshly brewed, sweet and cold, faintly like the summer days of my childhood. I close my eyes and take a deep breath. I say something I've never said to my mother, maybe not even when I was a little girl.

"Because I need help."

CHAPTER 11

Two Years Later

I AM RUSHING AROUND THE HOUSE, getting ready. Cal will be home in two hours, and I have those two hours to myself. On a Friday night, it's like heaven.

Amy jabbers in my ear, something about the orchestra, the one I've left. I still hear the gossip through Cal. Nikolai is still Nikolai. Amy is still concertmistress. Cal is still Cal, easy-going and happy just to be, so different from anyone I've ever known. I sit and pull out my violin, the phone trapped between my shoulder and my ear, and work on tightening the bow. I pluck a low G, and it resonates in my hand.

"How's teaching?" Amy asks, an abrupt shift of topic, and I can't help wondering if it's out of competitiveness. Her voice is soft and low, and I decide that it's concern.

I sigh. "Harder and more rewarding than I ever thought possible."

I teach music theory at the college and am a private music coach in my spare time. I have less spare time now than I ever have.

"I'm happy for you, Karen, really. You're so much happier now." She says this almost wistfully. I wonder if she wants this: my life with my little pseudo-family and upcoming wedding. I think back to how I used to be—lost, wandering, aimless—and feel a surge of gratitude.

The doorbell rings, and for one odd second, I assume it must be Cal, that he forgot his key. He stays here more often than not, but I know moving is in our future. I've never been particularly attached to this apartment, and truth be told, it seems to shrink by the day. I'm up and across the living room in a few steps. I open the door. On the other side stands a petite, dark-haired woman. She glances at me pensively and then around me, as if she's trying to see who is inside.

"Hi, can I help you?" I ask her, covering the mouthpiece with my hand. I don't see any brochures in her hand, so I can't imagine she's selling anything.

"I… do you have a minute? I'm Claire Barnes…" Her voice trails off, and she coughs. "You might not know me. Or maybe you do? I'm Greg's wife."

The bottom drops out of my stomach. I grip the phone in my hand, and my legs feel cold and numb. My head buzzes.

"I'm going to have to call you back," I say to Amy, and without waiting for a reply, I hang up.

"Greg's wife?" I ask, hoping for one second, one quick, fleeting flash, that I'm wrong.

"Greg Barnes," she says. "There's been a car accident."

Oh. Thank God. I have no idea who she's talking about. A quick wave of euphoria fills my chest. I want to cry. "I'm sorry. The only Greg I know is Greg Randolf. Are you sure you have the right place?"

Her face goes white, and she sways on her feet. I think for a moment that she's going to pass out. Then she does something entirely unexpected. She puts her hand to her forehead, and she laughs. "You're going to want to let me in."

I make coffee. She sits at my kitchen table, practically shrinking into the wooden chair. She hugs her bulky bag to her chest, and I try to study her without studying her. Her dark, almost black hair lies in kinks and curls down her back. Her face is pale, and her eyes are huge. She looks breakable, like a china doll. This is Greg's wife? No wonder he couldn't leave her.

"I'm sorry about the mess," I say, just for something to say. "I travel for work." A stretch of the truth—I sometimes accompany the orchestra to guest performances if my teaching schedule allows. I'm self-conscious of this woman, who probably has matching potholders and a full serving set for

Thanksgiving. My apartment is still bare. I pour two mugs of coffee, mismatched. I hand her one with a picture of a disheveled cat that says *I don't do mornings!* "You said there was an accident?"

"Two years ago, Greg was mugged and pushed into the path of an oncoming car. He was in a coma at St. Michael's until six months ago. When he woke up, he didn't remember anything, not his name, where he was from, nothing." She speaks slowly, twirling her spoon around her coffee mug. It sounds as though she's reading off of a script.

I cover my mouth with my hand, feeling sick. I take a deep breath and try to picture Greg, strong, tall, powerful Greg, hooked up to beeping machines and tubes with clear liquid, alone in a hospital bed mere miles away—for years—while I stayed here, moved on, dated Cal, mended things with Paula. *Oh, God, Paula will be back.* The back of my throat itches. "Is he okay?"

"Yes, sort of. He *will* be. Right now, his memory is spotty. He remembered your name, though. And mine and my children."

Children. Oh God, I'm going to throw up. I can feel it right in my throat, that watery, slippery back-of-the-mouth feeling. *Children. What were you doing with me, Greg?*

"Greg was married," I say stupidly, stalling for time. My mind races through possible responses but settles on blankness. I literally can't think. I need to get this woman out of my house. I need to think.

While You Were Gone

Greg has been a shadowy remembrance in my mind for two years, and he needs to stay that way—a vague figure, the way I thought of Claire when I first found that ring. I need them both to go back to being cardboard people. Not real. "It makes sense. I could never call him. He was always traveling, he said."

"How did you meet?"

I don't answer her right away. I remember Greg the night that Scott broke up with me, the night I lost my audition. "Where else? In a bar. He was here for work. It had to be... oh, close to three years ago now?" *The very best version of you.*

"You didn't know about his accident, then? The nurses said it was in the paper." She narrows her eyes at me, and I shift uncomfortably.

"The night he broke up with me was the last time I saw him," I say, knowing he didn't exactly break up with me. Well, not technically, but he didn't choose me, either. Now I know why. *Children.* I want so badly to ask: how many kids? Boys? I can see Greg with all boys, a whole football team of boys.

"What night was that?" Her voice is sharp, like a cop trying to trap a criminal. My face heats up; I can feel it crawl up the back of my neck.

"I don't know the date exactly. I guess it was late September..." I'm stalling, and she has those eyes trained on me, sharp as a tack. I don't know what she's looking for or expecting, but I know all her staring me down is making me nervous.

"September thirtieth?"

"Maybe? It was a Thursday night. I remember because I was leaving on Friday. I had a concert in New York. I cried the entire bus ride."

"Tell me everything. Please?" She pushes her shoulders back, flush against the wooden chair.

I feel sorry for her. I shouldn't feel angry, but I do. "I loved him. I thought he loved me. Or at least he said he did." One time. One time he told me he loved me. My vision swims.

"Then why did you break up? That night?"

I can't give her a good reason. Because I found out he was married? I already told her I didn't know he was married.

I remember Paula asking about Greg, and I'd just told her he moved to China, latching onto the story he offered me before I realized it was probably just a set-up for a way out. Even back then—in his fading voice through the phone late at night—he was trying to figure out how to end it but was too much of a coward for the truth.

I sit up straight, pushing my back against the chair, my hands folded in my lap. "His company was transferring him to China. Some executive position, a big promotion. He thought it was a great opportunity." I babble inanely. "I was a violinist in the Toronto Symphony Orchestra. I was trying for concertmistress, the youngest in the history of the TSO. He wanted me to go with him, but there was no way I could go. We decided to put our relationship... on hold."

She laughs and shakes her head. My story is thin enough to see through. She reaches over and touches my hand, her skin cool and soft. "Karen, there was no China. Greg was a bored, thirty-five-year-old man in a troubled marriage with a couple of kids in the suburbs of New Jersey."

The picture she paints of him, the way she sees him, is so drastically different than my vision. He *did* love her. I realize that now. The way she tosses that off as if it means nothing infuriates me. It occurs to me then that I knew Greg better than his wife of ten years. I've never believed in soul mates. They always seemed the stuff of fairy tales, Sandra Bullock movies, and romance novels.

I close my eyes. "He said he didn't have kids but that he'd wanted them."

I hear her suck in a deep breath like I've stabbed her. When I open my eyes, her black eyes are peering at me with bald hatred. "Do you still love him?" Her voice is mocking, almost singsong. In that moment, I hate her too. My body feels like it's vibrating with the hate.

I hold up my left hand, displaying Cal's diamond, and shake my head. "I called his cell over and over until one day, after a month or so, the recording said the phone had been disconnected. It took about a year for me to move on. I knew he was American. He said he was originally from Syracuse, but it hadn't mattered because he was never home.

I stopped trying after that and met a very nice trombone player. The wedding's in May."

She smirks at me, her head cocked to the side, this woman in my kitchen, with her china-doll face and her big black eyes. I feel small. I want to tell her, *I didn't know he was married.* Until, of course, I did. I need her to leave. I check the clock. Paula will be here any minute, and this woman cannot be here when Paula gets here. I can't even think about it. Paula and Claire facing off with my whole life between them? Panic rises, and I swallow the bile in my throat.

I stand up, go to the drawer in the kitchen, and rummage around the back of it until I find it. The picture strip with Greg, the one from the mall. When we were happy. I shove it at her, angrily. I need her to take it and leave. It's all I have left of Greg and me, not, of course, the only proof we ever existed at all, but the only thing available to me at that moment. I want to yell at her, "*get out, get out, get out.*" I'm standing, lording it over her, really, and I know it's cruel, but I can't help it. She needs to leave. Take the picture and leave.

She stares at it, dumbfounded, and says nothing for a long few moments. Then, softly, "He looks so happy."

"Well, Greg was a goofball." I almost laugh, thinking of all his jibing, our random question game, his singing in public, just walking down the street, singing. For a split second, I lose my focus, lost in the memory. She gives me the oddest look, almost as though she's frightened of me. She touches her hand to her forehead.

"I have to go." She stands up, leaves her coffee untouched on the table, and the picture strip flutters back to the tabletop. I rush her to the door. She turns, and giving one last look around the apartment, she says, "Good bye. It was nice meeting you." She shakes her head with a little laugh. I shut the door behind her and breathe out, my heart hammering the inside of my ribcage like bat wings.

I hear Paula in the hallway. She has Wyatt with her. They must even pass by Claire as she's leaving. I wonder if she looks at them, if she notices the little boy. If some maternal instinct pricks deep inside her, and she notices the brown of his eyes, the deep, cavernous brown that seemed to belong only to Greg.

I wonder if her children inherited that, too.

I hear Wyatt's excited voice talking over Paula, and I imagine his chubby hands flying. His words are gibberish still. He's nearly two, but he talks a blue streak. More than you'd think.

I open the door and scoop him up and kiss his sandy-blond hair, floppy and curly and smelling like sunscreen and lollipop. His sturdy little arms circle my neck, and he laughs into my ear, a gurgly bubbling. I step back and stare at his face, those wide brown eyes, mirror images of his daddy's.

I pull Paula inside and shut the door.

"What's the problem?" she asks, loud and irritated, and I wave her silent. As far as she knows, Wyatt's American daddy is living in China, and Wyatt is safe here, in Canada. Before he was born, I used to dream about Greg coming back. He loved me, he'd say. He missed me. Then, when I started seeing Cal, I'd wake up in the night, panicked and sweating at the thought that he'd come back and take it all away. Never did I imagine he was mere miles away, simply sleeping. My arms gooseflesh.

International parental rights are complicated. He could fight for custody. *Custody.* Take my Wyatt, on select weekends and holidays, back to the States with him, to his wife, his kids. Tears pool in my eyes. He knows nothing about Wyatt. Nothing about how he hates loud noises or loves ambulances but only if they're a block away. He doesn't know that he hates spaghetti and any red sauce but loves white pizza and eats spinach, but only on toast. He doesn't know that two of Wyatt's toes on each foot are webbed—are Greg's toes webbed?—or that his thumbs are slightly different shapes. Greg doesn't know how he likes to curl my hair around his index finger when he's tired. Sometimes, he talks in his sleep, his hand touching his own mouth, and I think about genetics and how it's amazing. I try not to panic about all the things I don't know, heart disease and genetic disorders and cancer history.

I don't want to know those things. Someday, Wyatt might ask about his father, and I'll decide then: is a father the person who raised you or the person who gave you life in the first place?

"Are you okay?" Paula asks. "You're white as a ghost."

I nod and kiss Wyatt's cheeks, wet with drool and tears and red from the wind. He laughs and slaps at me with his chubby hands, his toothy grin inches from my face.

His smile is so much like Greg's that, sometimes, it takes my breath away.

If Claire had seen him, really looked at him, she'd surely know. Anyone could see it. I put him down, and he scampers to Paula. Her arm snakes protectively around his shoulders.

At the kitchen window, I part the curtains. A small, dark car is leaving, making a left out of the parking lot. I wonder if it's her, if Greg is with her. I wonder if they'll be back. On the table, from the glossy picture strip, Greg's wide smile grins back at me. For a second, and only a second, the pain of losing him is fresh all over again, a sharp knife twist right in my center, and I can't catch my breath. I thought she would have taken the picture, but she left it, tossed carelessly on the table. I pick it up gingerly between my thumb and forefinger and hover it over the trash. I could do that: throw it away, shove it down under the paper plates with waffles and syrup and Wyatt's leftover banana. The whole thing would be over, almost like it never happened.

Except it did happen. Wyatt plops on the floor

and pulls out a bin of Duplos from under the couch, and I watch his chubby hands stack and click those bright little boxes together, his mind analyzing and compiling and solving problems. One day, he'll ask me where his daddy is. This picture is all I have left of Greg, aside from Wyatt himself. The picture is all I have left to give him.

I look at it one last time, the crinkled eyes, the glinty glasses, his lips against my cheek—I swear I can almost feel them.

What I have now, with Cal, is so real, so honest. We fell in love when Wyatt was a newborn, the intensity of baby-mama fog matched only by my growing admiration for the man who cared for a baby who wasn't his. My love for Greg was whirlwind and breathless but packaged in half truths and self-delusion. My love for Cal has grown organically to the steady swell of a low-tide ocean and just as expansive.

I open the junk drawer, the one with the garlic press, the lemon juicer, and the apple slicer that Cal got me for my birthday, a joke after picking up after a rash of abandoned cores. I shove the picture of Greg and me behind all the debris of domestic life, those shiny things you never use and sometimes forget you even have.

ACKNOWLEDGMENTS

First, thanks to the many readers who made *Thought I Knew You* successful enough to warrant a sequel(-ish). Thanks to everyone who asked, "But what is Greg's story?" for inspiring me to write it. I even thank those of you who hated Greg with such vitriol that you extended this challenge.

Thanks to Red Adept Publishing for the always-thorough, always-professional editing, cover art, formatting, and friendship. It's always a joy, and at this point, it feels warm and comfy in this house. Jessica and Karen, it was fun working together to bring Karen's story to life.

Thank you to my outstanding first readers:

Elizabeth Buhman, who catches literally everything (I smile with gritted teeth at your notes). I can't imagine I'll ever write or publish anything without your eyes on it first. You are one of my favorite people, but you know that.

Thank you to Kimberly Giarratano, who says "more

conflict," and I oblige because she knows what she's talking about.

Thanks to Mary Fan, who corrected my bumbling attempts at research on the violin, symphonies, and all things musical.

Thanks to Ann Garvin and Sonja Yoerg, who read this manuscript and offered their thoughts, notes, and ramblings. Not to mention wonderful praise, which I promptly displayed everywhere.

Lastly, thanks to the real Karen, who is nothing at all like the fictional Karen but who has always encouraged me to write my first novel, so much so that I named a seemingly throwaway character after her (only to bring her back five years later).

Thanks to my mom. She reads everything I write and sometimes forgets to tell me when she's done. She drives around with my books in her car and sells them to her friends. She's my Number One Fan.

Finally, thanks to Chip, who is always ignored while I write. He accommodates my writing schedule, which is not a schedule at all because I'm erratic and scatterbrained and unorganized. He does more housework than your average husband and picks up all my half-empty water cups. You do all my laundry, you make me laugh, you order my chaos.

ABOUT THE AUTHOR

New York Times Bestselling Author Kate Moretti lives in Pennsylvania with her husband, two kids, and a dog. She's worked in the pharmaceutical industry for ten years as a scientist, and has been an avid fiction reader her entire life.

She enjoys traveling and cooking, although with two kids, a day job, and writing, she doesn't get to do those things as much as she'd like.

Her lifelong dream is to buy an old house with a secret passageway.

CPSIA information can be obtained
at www.ICGtesting.com
Printed in the USA
BVHW030216071221
623411BV00004B/175